WHAT IN THE SAM HILL?

KAREN BARBARO POTOCHICK

Print ISBN: 978-1-54397-920-6

eBook ISBN: 978-1-54397-921-3

INTRODUCTION

My name is Sam Hill, and I'm an average twelve-year-old girl in a not-so-average family. By average, I mean a little taller than my friends at 5'5" tall already, average weight I guess—I'm not sure because I never weigh myself—and shoulder-length brown hair with hazel eyes. That seems about average, but before I go any further with this story, there's a few not-so-average-more-like-weird facts to know about me. But more about that later.

CHAPTER ONE

"Mmmm." I love when Mom is going through a cooking phase. This was the best of all phases. Way better than the gardening phase, the cleaning phase, and the fix-all-the-stuff-that's-broken phase!

The morning that my "official" career as an amateur detective began, I woke to the smell of breakfast cooking and sat up slowly looking around for the clock. "Seven o'clock. Ugh." My mom liked us all to have breakfast together before my dad went to his job as a "real" detective for the local police department, and homeschooling began. I swung my legs over the side of the bed and sat there for a second, not quite ready to embrace the day.

So, besides my mom who's weird, there are a few other things to know about me which are also weird. First, I'm homeschooled. That's weird. Not sure why my parents just couldn't send me to school like normal people. But they had a list of reasons for homeschooling, so I was letting it go... for now. Second, my parents met at a karate tournament a thousand years ago when they were "young," so they both had a bunch of black belts and taught martial arts as a hobby. So. Weird. Third, we had a dojo in our house.

A DOJO IS A PLACE WHERE PEOPLE TRAIN IN MARTIAL ARTS.

It's a big padded room with mats on the floor and on the wall, that looks a little bit like a place where the mentally insane go to hang out, except with colorful mats. I guess that part was kind of cool. So, even though my parents kept a pretty low profile in the neighborhood, they did teach some classes to close friends, neighbors, and family. And when the dojo wasn't being used as a dojo, it was just a fun padded room for us to play in. And fourth, I recently decided to be a private detective, so I spent my spare time looking for neighborhood crimes to solve.

My parents have been pushing me to study the martial arts ever since I could walk. Until recently, I didn't feel the need for martial arts. But ever since "the episode," I had renewed interest.

CHAPTER TWO

"Sam," my mom bellowed from the kitchen, "Come to breakfast."

"Just a minute," I yelled back. I looked at my tiny closet where my even tinier wardrobe was housed. Unfortunately, I knew I'd inherited some of my mom's limited sense of style, but because my mom chose to be a stay-at-home mom, I was at the mercy of her also limited budget.

I walked over to the door to shut it while I changed and glanced into the kitchen where my mom stood with her back to me. I guess I got my averageness from her too. She was still taller than me at about 5'8", average weight although she always seemed to be on a diet, and short brown hair and hazel eyes like me.

I GLANCED AT THE CUT-OFF SHORTS AND T-SHIRT SHE WAS WEARING AND GROANED AS I TURNED BACK TO MY CLOSET.

I finally settled on the usual—jeans and a t-shirt—quickly changed my clothes before my five-year-old brother, Wyatt, could come bursting into the room. He was a 4-ft-tall, 50-pound ball of energy that was usually running toward, or away, from something in the house. Boys were weird, so he was a bit of a mystery to me.

I opened the door and walked down to the kitchen, where my mom was still standing at the counter squinting at a cookbook. "Uh, oh," I thought, "This can't be good."

I made my way to the table where my dad was reading the paper and my younger sister, Frankie, was reading *Harry Potter* again for like the tenth time. She is two years younger than me, but almost as tall and really skinny. Her hair is a little bit lighter than mine, but she has hazel eyes, the same color as mine and Wyatt's. She kept reading as I entered the room, while Wyatt amused himself with some army guys. My mom made grunting noises as she continued to struggle with the recipe.

"Well, this ought to be interesting," I thought to myself. But I knew from experience that in the case of my mom's food obsessions, interesting didn't always mean good. The last time she got obsessed with something, our house smelled like cabbage soup for weeks. To this day, I couldn't smell cabbage soup without my gag reflex kicking in. I poured myself some orange juice and waited. I grabbed my iPod earbuds so I wouldn't have to hear what types of ingredients were going into the muffins. This would increase my chances of actually eating them. At least she was learning to make a back-up food just in case, and had some pancake mix on standby.

"Only a few more minutes," my mom called over her shoulder.

MY DAD PUT DOWN HIS PAPER JUST IN TIME TO SEE ME PULL MY IPOD OUT OF MY POCKET. "NO ELECTRONICS AT THE TABLE, YOUNG LADY."

I wasn't sure if it was his job as a detective or his role as a Sensei at our home dojo that made everything sound like a command. But either way, my dad wasn't really one to argue with, so I put it away.

Frankie snickered. I glared at her. Twerp. "No books either, right, Dad?" I said, hoping to get her in trouble.

"Right," he agreed. "The breakfast table is a place where we gather as a family, and do what we used to do in the old days..." he looked at us expectantly, hoping neither one of us would notice as he sheepishly hid his newspaper under his chair.

"What's that?" Frankie asked.

I gave her one of my most withering looks that said, "Ugh, how could you be so stupid," hoping my dad wouldn't ask me to fill in the blank, because I really had no idea what he was talking about either.

"Talk," he said. "We used to talk to each other. You know, without the help of text messaging?" We looked at him like he had two heads. "It's when you open your mouth, and words come out? Hopefully, in some kind of a sentence pattern that makes sense?" He waited.

I looked at Frankie. She stared back at me. Neither one of us wanted to encourage this new ritual. After what seemed like an eternity, I looked back at my dad, who leaned forward in anticipation.

"I GOT NOTHIN'," I SAID AND SHRUGGED.

Luckily, before we could engage in this new practice, my mom put the basket of warm muffins on the table, next to the bacon and eggs. "Dig in, everyone," she said as she sat down.

"Sam, would you like one?" My mom was looking at me expectantly.

"Uh," I hesitated, wondering if this was a trick question. Without waiting for an answer, my mom passed the basket of muffins, and waited expectantly for everyone to take one.

Muffins served, glasses filled, and reading material put away, my mom sat down at the table to join the family. She noticed that while everyone was slowly putting butter on their muffins, but no one was actually eating. We all seemed to be waiting for her to take the first bite.

"What's wrong," she asked looking around the table.

My dad looked at me. "Don't look at me," I said, "She's your wife."

"What's that supposed to mean?" he asked.

"I feel I can speak on behalf of the young and innocent," I gestured Frankie and Wyatt at this point, who for a change didn't object to being called young, "And say that we'd like to bestow the honor of testing out this new recipe on you, Dad."

"Me, why me?" he said, suddenly looking a little nervous and even a bit frightened.

"DO I HAVE TO REMIND YOU OF LAST YEAR'S OMELET INCIDENT?" I SAID.

"Oh brother," my mom interjected. "How melodramatic can you be? It wasn't that bad."

"Mom," I reminded her, "You can't even say the word 'asparagus' to Frankie without her breaking out into hives. Watch this," I turned to Frankie and gave her the look, "Asparagus!" I said in my best spooky whisper voice.

Right on cue, Frankie shuddered, gagged, and immediately looked at her arms to convince her mom that there were huge, hideous spots. "See," I turned to my mom victoriously.

My mom rolled her eyes. She unwrapped her muffin and raised it to her mouth. She hesitated ever so briefly, shut her eyes, and quickly took a bite. We leaned forward and waited.

My mom grinned. "Not bad," she said, "Not bad at all."

With visible relief, we all began to eat. My dad got up to get another cup of coffee. I think he was stalling to see if anyone would have any delayed reaction to the latest recipe. I know he was working on some cases involving a string of robberies that had been occurring in the area, so he was trying not to get poisoned at home.

"So," Mom said, putting another bite of muffin in her mouth, "My tennis partner, Mrs. Marlin, took her diamond engagement ring to be cleaned the other day, and found out it was a fake!"

Suddenly, I was interested. This sounded like the beginning of another case!

My dad looked back at my mom blankly. "What do you mean fake?"

Who knew this breakfast was going to be so interesting? I waited for my mom to answer my dad's question so I could determine if this was another case for me.

My first case happened almost by accident a few weeks ago. In fact, it could have turned ugly for me, and I hadn't really told my mom, or my dad for that matter, all the details. But the day had started just like any other day. Well, almost any other day.

CHAPTER THREE

Luckily, two days before the morning of "the incident," we'd had a class that went over a very useful technique. But not before some techniques that I deemed not-so-useful.

"So, breakfalls, huh?" I glanced at my training partner, Catherine, and then back to the mat.

It was 9 a.m. on a Saturday morning, and class was full for some reason. I looked around at the other students of various ages. Didn't anyone believe in sleeping in? Why couldn't class be held at the crack of, say noon, for example? Breakfalls were so much harder on an empty stomach.

I stood there wondering why in the world I was there in the first place. Well, I knew *why* I was there. My mom taught the class. I had no way out. It didn't seem to matter whether or not I liked it. I was trapped. Catherine, on the other hand, had a choice. Why was she there? Ugh. So many questions.

"A BREAKFALL IS A WAY TO BREAK YOUR FALL WITHOUT GETTING HURT," MY MOM WAS SAYING.

"Yuh, huh. Like if you got knocked down, or thrown, like in a judo tournament, or out of a moving car. Two things that would happen, say… never," I thought, but would never say out loud. I continued to stare at the ground, wondering why anyone would voluntarily throw themselves down onto it. I looked up to find my mom, or Sensei Hill as I had to call her in class, staring at me.

"How's that breakfall coming, Sam?" my mom asked. I was just standing there staring at the mat that I was supposed to throw myself down on, and it just didn't seem like a good idea. Catherine had just dropped to the ground and executed what looked like a perfect breakfall. Great. A natural. Now I was even more insecure. My mom stared at me staring at the mat. "You have to visualize success. Imagine yourself doing the technique perfectly." She'd said this a thousand times. "Try doing it from a squatting position," she said. "That way the ground won't seem so far away." She got down in a squat position and rolled backward to execute a breakfall[1].

Alright, that didn't look so hard. I squatted, feeling like a sumo wrestler, only less limber, and rolled back and to my right and hit the mat as hard as I could with my right hand.

"Perfect," my mom said smiling. "See, there's a martial artist inside you after all! Now, go write it down, so you don't forget." They made all of the students keep a notebook, so we remembered all the details of a technique. And, in my case, just for added fun, they made me retype my hand-written notes. I think that's because we had to turn in our notes at testing time and my hand writing was slightly illegible. Oh, and I guess the writing it, rewriting it, reading it, and doing it helps you remember it.

I smiled back at her as I grabbed my notebook. I finished my notes just in time to hear my mom bellow, "Get a partner, it's time to practice wrist escapes. Let's start with a pry bar!"

*FOR MORE INFORMATION ON THIS TECHNIQUE, SEE MY NOTEBOOK AT THE BACK OF THE BOOK.

1

CHAPTER FOUR

I snapped out of my daydream, and my dad was still waiting for my mom to reply.

"What about her ring?" he repeated.

"She said that the only time she ever takes it off is when she plays tennis."

"And?"

"Well, isn't that one of the cases you're working on?"

"You know I can't discuss any of these cases with you, right? Especially not in front of you-know-who." He glanced in my direction.

"Who? Me? Why not? Maybe I could help solve it! You know I'm starting my own detective business, right?" I looked at my mom for help. "I already helped the Batemans get their dog back after all! I even used the pry bar technique you showed us in class!"

My mom's eyes opened wide. My dad looked at me, then at her, then at me again. "Excuse me?"

"Uh oh," suddenly I remembered that I hadn't actually shared some of the details with them, knowing what their reaction would be.

"UM, WELL, UH, ER," I STAMMERED. "IT'S A FUNNY STORY, REALLY."

"I need a good laugh, please proceed." He leaned back in his chair, crossed his arms, and waited for the details.

Where to begin that wouldn't get me grounded for life?

CHAPTER FIVE

My parents were looking at me intently. I swallowed, "Um...well, you remember when you taught us the pry bar technique, right, Mom?"

"Yes." She offered no other details, clearly not wanting to be implicated in whatever came next. "So?"

"WELL, IT CAME IN REALLY HANDY AND I EXECUTED IT PERFECTLY; YOU WOULD HAVE BEEN PROUD!"

I stopped waiting to see if they were going to heap any praise in my direction. Apparently not.

"It all started with a hunch, or gut instinct." I looked at my dad as I said this. When he taught self-defense, he always said, "Gut instinct is 99% accurate, so if the hairs on the back of your neck stand up, you need to pay attention," so I thought if I mentioned this, he would know I was paying attention and any punishment resulting from this story would be less severe. By the look on his face, I'm not sure this theory was paying off. "So," I continued, "When the Batemans' dog went missing, I started to notice things. I can't help it. That's how I roll. I'm observant."

They didn't look impressed. I kept going. "First off, the Batemans had a show dog. A Samoyed to be exact. This incredibly furry animal is a large breed of Russian herding dog and could cost as much as $11,000!"

"I KNOW," I PAUSED AT THE LOOKS ON THEIR FACES. "RIDICULOUS. BUT EVERYBODY'S GOT TO HAVE A HOBBY I GUESS.

Anyway, that's the first detail that made me think it was dognapped, rather than a dog runaway. And second, the guy across the street was not exactly subtle about his interest in the dog. He just kept staring at it. Worst dognapper ever. Third, the dog was pure white and weighed about 70 pounds, so if it just ran away, it would be pretty easy to spot."

My parents exchanged glances. Unfortunately, I was not well-versed in what these glances meant, and all I knew is that I was still in trouble. "When poor old Snowball went missing, I just knew Mr. Smith took him, and I also knew there was only a short window of time to retrieve the dog before it was gone forever. So I came up with a plan to prove that I was right. Admittedly, it could have gone better, but it all worked out in the end."

"How did you know his name was Mr. Smith?" my dad asked. "Didn't he just move in recently? I didn't even know his name."

"I looked in his mailbox, of course," I said.

"You did what?!"

"What? All of our mailboxes are in the same spot." I paused. "It was an accident. Sort of. It's not like I took anything."

"WE NEED TO HAVE A SERIOUS TALK ABOUT TRESPASSING, YOUNG LADY."

He was starting to turn red. "Continue."

"Well, I was listening to my gut instinct," I tried again, "Just like you taught us." I thought a little buttering up couldn't hurt. No reaction. "So, when the Batemans' $11,000 Samoyed, Snowball, disappeared," I repeated, "I knew we only had 24 hours before the dog was gone forever."

"Where did you come up with that statistic?" he asked.

"TV?" I was surprised he didn't know this already.

"Yeah, that's for human kidnapping cases. Not dogs. But go on."

"Well, I had been noticing the way Mr. Smith was staring at their dog for a couple of days leading up to the disappearance." I looked back and forth from my mom to my dad, not sure how they would take the rest of this story. "The first time, I was actually over at the Batemans' playing with Courtney, and I noticed him staring from across the street." Courtney, the oldest of the Bateman kids was exactly my age and we had gotten to be friends through the Girl Scout troop we both belonged to. We had been playing in the backyard with the dog, and Mr. Smith had actually come out on his porch to take a picture of the dog. I didn't think it was weird until the second time I saw him. "Then, I saw him take a picture of the dog when Andrea was walking him around the block," I said indicating the middle Bateman child who was roughly the same age as Frankie. "And then, as if that wasn't enough I saw him in his living room window with a pair of binoculars! Now that's unusual, wouldn't you agree?"

Ignoring the questions, my dad asked, "And you didn't think to say anything then?" He was using his detective voice.

"I'm just a kid," I said, "No one listens to me." I kept going, "And, when the Batemans called to see if we had seen their dog, I just knew it was him. So, I noticed that he had closed all the blinds in his house, and I also noticed that he had put tape and newspaper over the basement windows."

"And how exactly did you find that out?" My dad was starting to raise his voice.

"Um…I snuck into his backyard, and looked?" I was speaking slowly and carefully as if that would help me avoid a potential lifetime grounding. My mom looked horrified, partly because she thought she knew the whole story, and partly because she just realized she was about to hear some details she was unaware of before. When I said I hadn't told her all the details of the "episode," I meant I hadn't really told her anything at all.

My dad looked like he didn't know if he should ground me immediately, or wait until I finished my story, but I was in it now, so I continued. "I peered into one of the basement windows where it looked like the paper had come loose, and I could see a big dog cage, so I knew I was right."

At this statement, my dad actually put his head down on the table. I glanced at my mom to see if I should continue. I took a deep breath. I was not looking forward to their reaction when I told them what came next.

CHAPTER SIX

"I had just come home from snooping, er, I mean looking, in Mr. Smith's yard, and it had only been a couple of hours since the Batemans had called to see if we had seen their dog anywhere, so I knew he didn't have time to get rid of Snowball. He still had to have him in his house. I had to act quick." I paused just in case either of my parents needed to ask a question, but they both seemed speechless at this point. I wasn't sure if that was good or bad, so I plowed ahead. "It had been raining all morning, but stopped about an hour previously, and you," I pointed at my mom, "were wrapped up in some kind of science experiment in the bathroom with Frankie and Wyatt." My mom glanced at my dad. This was never good. Parents occasionally communicated with some unspoken language, and from experience I knew that us kids never benefited from it. "I knew I had a window of opportunity." I stopped. "Everybody okay?" I looked from one parent to the other. "Nothing personal, but you guys don't look so good."

MY MOM GLARED AT ME. "JUST CONTINUE SO WE CAN GET TO THE END OF THIS HORROR STORY."

Confused, I continued. "So, I decided to create a Welcome-to-the-Neighborhood basket. I got a basket and put a bunch of welcome stuff in it. You know, a roll of toilet paper, one giant dog biscuit, a few cookies, and a couple of Keurig k-cups."

"A roll of toilet paper?" My mom looked like she was about to give me a lesson in neighborhood etiquette but thought better of it.

"Yep. Perfect, right?" My mom looked at my dad and shrugged. "All I needed him to do was open the door, so I could look inside and see if I could see, smell, or hear anything." At this point, my dad pushed his chair back from the table and got a glass of water.

"I knocked on his door, and waited for him to answer," I said. "When he came to the door, I just said, 'Hi, my name is Sam. We saw that you moved in recently and we just wanted to welcome you to the neighborhood.'"

Now my mom's head went down on the table. "The man in the doorway just stared at me." As I told my mom and dad this story, I remembered that he was about 40-ish, and kind of average. He was so average, in fact, that I wasn't even sure what color his eyes were. He was shorter than my dad, so not quite six feet tall, and other than that, he had absolutely no distinguishing characteristics whatsoever. I remembered it like it was yesterday.

CHAPTER SEVEN

"'Uh…,' I stood on his porch staring at him. This was not going well. At this point, it was usually customary, I thought, for the other person to speak. But no such luck. 'So,' I extended the basket. 'Here you go.' I held the basket closer to him, but far enough out that he would have to open the door more than the fraction that he had it open now to retrieve it."

"He stared stupidly at the dog bone."

"'It's for your dog. I thought I saw a dog in your backyard the other day, and I didn't want to forget the little pooch, so I wanted to make him feel welcome too.' I looked expectantly at the neighbor. I held out my hand, 'And you are…' I waited."

"'I don't have a dog,' he said nervously, glancing around. But, quicker than I would have imagined possible, he opened his door a little wider, snatched the basket out of my hand, and was closing the door without another word."

I shuddered, remembering the incident.

"IF IT WASN'T FOR MY EQUALLY LIGHTNING QUICK REFLEXES," I SAID, "THE OPPORTUNITY WOULD HAVE BEEN LOST."

I sized up my mom and dad for any reaction to the story. Nothing so far. "Going back to a stalling technique I developed at home when I want to avoid a subject, I doubled over in a fit of coughing." I hoped I wasn't violating any kid code by divulging this technique to my parents, but this story was not helping my chances of not being grounded.

Under his breath, my dad mumbled, "I'm surprised you didn't just tell him a story."

"Whatdya mean by that?" I asked.

"UGH, NOTHING," HE GLANCED AT HIS WATCH, "KEEP GOING. I'M INVESTED NOW."

"As I was saying, I coughed, put my hand on the door to keep it from closing and leaned on it as if I had lost my balance. Then I just pushed it open a little farther. Mr. Smith was caught off guard. With the door opened wider now, I was able to see into the living room behind him before he could recover and close the door again. What I saw, felt, and smelled confirmed my suspicions."

"Which was?" My dad seemed mildly curious, but still annoyed.

"Well, it was the smell of wet dog!" Now my parents surely had to react. They just exchanged glances. "During the time when Snowball had been taken it was raining cats and dogs, no pun intended. He would have been soaked. The smell was unmistakable. And, the Batemans' yard is muddy because of the landscaping they're doing. The dog's feet are always covered in mud. I've heard them complain about it before."

"So?" my dad said.

"Well, there were muddy dog prints all over Mr. Smith's carpet!" I stopped triumphantly. "And, before he could close the door, I was able to see the computer screen from the door. On the screen was a picture of Snowball, along with a description and a price tag of $11,000." At this point in the story, I'm not going to lie, both my parents looked horrified.

"This is where it could have gone better, I guess," I paused. "I think he knew I'd seen something and asked me to come in with the basket. I said, 'No thanks,' but he reached out and grabbed my arm. As he grabbed my arm, he said, 'let me get you a drink of water for that cough.'"

I shuddered remembering how scared I was. "So, without even think-ing, I stepped in slightly, putting him slightly off balance, pushed my elbow to his elbow and my wrist against his thumb. A flawless pry-bar!"

I stopped to see if either of them wanted to congratulate me. They didn't. On I trudged. "And, it worked perfectly. Before I knew what hap-pened, my arm was out of his grasp and he had a look of bewilderment on his face. He reached out again, but after I mumbled, 'no, thanks,' I rushed off the porch. I glanced back at the porch where he was staring after me, and rushed in the direction of home, trying not to look like I was running. Now that I'd caught him red-handed, the window of opportunity was clos-ing. I had to move fast."

I finished my story and looked at my mom and dad. "I think you know the rest," I said. "Mom and I called the police and told them everything..."

Both of my parents gave me a look that said, "Really? Everything?"

"Well, the important details anyway, and the rest, as they say, is his-tory!" After a few more minutes of stunned silence, I figured I might as well go for it. "So, about Mrs. Marlin's diamond ring. I say we go to the Tennis Club and do some sleuthing! Who's with me?"

CHAPTER EIGHT

After a few minutes of Silent Parental Communication, the worst of all parental communications really, my dad left for work, leaving my mom to come up with the appropriate punishment for the story I had just told. Apparently, there were a number of crimes against humanity, or at least crimes against the rules of the house, that couldn't be left unpunished. I took my place at the kitchen table as my mom busied herself cleaning. This is what she did when she was mad. When she was really mad, our house was usually spotless!

She finally stopped and looked at me. "Alright, young lady..." she began. By this time Frankie and Wyatt had wandered into the room and were staring at my mom and me. They recognized the tone of voice, so knew enough not to approach, but weren't quite sure what had happened. Wyatt looked to Frankie for instructions, but she was just frozen in place. Following her lead, he just stood there. I wasn't sure I'd ever seen him this still.

"GO CHANGE INTO YOUR GI AND GET INTO THE DOJO."

She turned her back on me and began to prepare a lesson to keep them busy.

I slunk off to my room to change. Punishment by workout. The worst of all punishments. I knew from past experience that whatever she was conjuring up for me was going to be (1) good for me, (2) was going to teach me a lesson, and (3) would result in my not being able to walk without muscle pain for at least three days. The good news was that I was about to become an expert in something.

"Mom," I began trying to reason with her. "Do you really think you should be using martial arts as a punishment if it's something you want me to end up liking?"

She turned to face me. Maybe this wasn't the best time to try to negotiate. "Well, Samantha," she began. Uh, oh. She was using my given name. Not good. "Don't think of it as punishment, think of it as preparation for, and prevention of, future dumbness." She smiled a knowing smile. The conversation was over.

CHAPTER NINE

Two hours later, I hobbled into the kitchen where my sister and brother were already working on their lesson of the day. My mom dropped a pile of books and papers in front of me and handed me a pencil. I took it silently and waited for instructions. Sometimes I knew better than to open my mouth.

"GET OUT YOUR MATH BOOKS, EVERYONE," SHE CALLED.

We all retrieved our books and once we were all working on various math assignments, she looked to the calendar to determine what the next subject was. Mondays included gym, so depending on the weather, we either went outside for an activity, or went to the Tennis Club.

I glanced outside. It was late April, so in Michigan it could either be snowing, or it could be 80 degrees. And, sometimes these things could seem to happen on the same day. This day was somewhere in the middle, so this afternoon's activities were more mood dependent than weather dependent.

I looked outside. The grass and tress had finally started to go from wintery brown to springy green. The trees had buds on them, and the grass looked like it might actually be getting long enough to mow. It was about 60 degrees, warmish for April, but the sun was shining, and the birds were singing.

"Alright, everybody," my mom said, glancing up at the clock. "Grab your tennis stuff and let's go to the club!"

Awesome! Despite my two-hour workout, I was looking forward to going to the club. After all, this would be the perfect opportunity to snoop around the club and find out more about Mrs. Marlin's ring!

CHAPTER TEN

I raced to grab my tennis stuff. "Yippee!" Frankie and Wyatt obviously felt the same way and scrambled for their tennis equipment before our mom could change her mind. This was a rare treat. Usually her idea of a gym class was the martial arts class she taught in the evenings to the neighborhood kids, so this was a step up, at least for me. All three of us lined up at the door with our tennis rackets in record time.

My mom pulled out of the driveway and headed down our street toward the tennis courts. Less than five minutes later we arrived at the club and piled out of the car.

I looked around to see if there was anyone I knew at the club. It was the middle of a school day, so I wasn't very hopeful, but occasionally if there was an early release day at the local school, I would see some kids from the neighborhood up here, so I wouldn't be stuck hanging out with my family. No such luck today, though.

"Ugh," I sighed. Out loud, I think.

"What?" My mom looked at me curiously. "I thought you liked tennis?"

"I do," I said. I just wish I could play it with my friends, I added silently.

"Oh?" She didn't sound convinced. "C'mon then. This should be fun," she added.

"Maybe after we play for a while, we can go look for Mrs. Marlin?" I said this tentatively, trying to judge her response.

She paused. "Maybe."

Well, that was better than a flat out "No." I guess I could endure a little tennis if it meant I got to snoop around the club later.

"Alright, you guys," she said, "Let's go play tennis." She marched off in the direction of the courts. We all trailed behind her looking like a bunch of baby ducks following their mom. Thank goodness no one was here to see this.

We continued to walk in a straight line past the swimming pool and cut through the basketball court that separated us from the tennis courts. We usually had to go around to avoid the boys playing hoops, but at this time of day, it was not in use and we could cut through the center. I glanced up at the track on the upper level that surrounded the court. No one was running today. The rooms that were on the second level also seemed vacant, even though they occasionally housed a daytime birthday party, or a teen event of some kind. There were several rooms upstairs of various sizes that could hold from five to thirty kids, but today it was pretty quiet.

We arrived at the courts and put our things in the center of one of them.

"Wait for the bounce and then swing," my mom started by lobbing balls to Wyatt. Frankie and I found a court of our own to practice on.

"HERE IT COMES AGAIN," SHE SAID TO WYATT. "IT'S GOING TO BOUNCE, THEN SWING. READY? OK, BOUNCE...SWING!"

Wyatt moved his tennis racket from the down position by his right leg, up to his left shoulder, and swung like a baseball bat. I had to admit, he had pretty good hand–eye coordination. Even though his swing was totally wrong, and he was hitting with the thin edge of the racket rather than the face, he was connecting every time. I shook my head and turned my attention back to my own game. I couldn't hit the ball like that in a million years, so even though my mom was trying to correct his swing, he was actually hitting the ball harder and farther that the rest of us.

"Ok, one more time. Point your feet that way." My mom pointed in the direction of the other courts. "Now, hold your racket so the strings are facing me. Watch your sister."

"Girls," she called. "Come over here and help me for a second."

My mom pointed at Frankie, who was doing everything she told Wyatt to do. "Now, watch Frankie hit the ball. Bounce, hit." She smiled at Frankie who was willingly being the guinea pig in this experiment. Lightly she tossed the ball to Frankie who hit it perfectly.

"See? Now you do it. Bounce...hit." Again, Wyatt started out perfectly then raised his racket to his shoulder to go for the big swing. And, again he hit it with the rim. "Almost," she said. She grabbed his racket and held it with the strings in the right direction. "Like this," she said. She did a couple of practice swings with him. "Now Sam is going to toss a couple of balls to us to try it out." She looked at me expectantly.

I put down my racket and grabbed a couple of balls. Together, my mom standing behind him holding his racket, they hit the ball perfectly. "See how easy that was? Now you do it." Putting his tennis racket to the down position while I picked up another ball, my mom backed up slightly.

"Ok, Sam, throw it." I hesitated.

"Are you sure you don't want to back up some more?" I asked her.

"Just throw it," she said.

I tossed the ball to Wyatt. True to form, he picked his racket up, put it back on his shoulder and swung as hard as he could.

Crack! It was the loudest sound I ever heard as the racket connected with its target.

Unfortunately, it wasn't the ball. It was my mom's nose!

CHAPTER ELEVEN

"Holy SHHHNIKES!" my mom shouted at the top of her lungs as the racket connected with her face. Not even sure what had happened, she dropped in a heap to the ground.

"Mom?! Are you okay?" both Frankie and I rushed over to where she knelt with her head touching the ground. Wyatt, sensing panic, immediately started wailing knowing he was in trouble, but not really sure why.

We looked at the ground underneath my mom's head. Frankie and I looked at each other, not sure what to do.

"Do you think she's dead?" Frankie asked me, rather calmly.

I ROLLED MY EYES. "SERIOUSLY? THIS IS HOW YOU'D REACT IF MOM WERE DEAD?" I SHOOK MY HEAD. "OF COURSE, SHE'S NOT DEAD. CAN'T YOU HEAR HER MOANING?"

Just then, my mom lifted her head off the ground. From where her hand was positioned under her nose, we could see a steady stream of blood. "Do you think one of you girls could stop debating your reaction to my untimely death and get me a towel or something?" Frankie and I bit our lips to keep from smiling. She sounded silly with her nose all plugged up like that. Wisely, I didn't point this out at the time.

I tried to assess my mom's injuries. Frankie kept repeating, "Mom, are you okay?" but it was muffled under the din of Wyatt's wailing.

"Frankie, go get napkins." I directed her, more to give her something else to do than for the actual napkins. "Wyatt, be quiet!!" He was really starting to crank up the volume since everyone seemed to be ignoring him.

"Mom, can you look up?" I wasn't used to being the adult, but someone had to be, and since my mom was preoccupied with bleeding and all, it seemed like the job fell to me.

My mom shook her head a little and looked up. "Tell me if there are any cuts on my face. Is my eye still in the socket?" She looked up slowly, in time to see me rolling my eyes again. "What?" she sounded annoyed.

"Aren't we being a little melodramatic, mom?" Honestly, one little whack to the face. And she was always telling *me* to "man up." I guess the shoe was on the other foot now.

She took her hands away from her nose. I gasped, "Yikes."

"What?"

"Nothing." Not if you don't mind looking like the creature from the black lagoon, I added silently. Holy crap! He really hit her hard. "It looks fine," I added, but reached desperately for the napkins that Frankie had returned with.

"I need a mirror," she said looking around to see how far the office was. "And," she continued, "I need to get this bleeding stopped. C'mon," she said to all three of us. Still holding her nose, and still bleeding, she walked like a zombie from *Night of the Living Dead* and made her way to the snack bar which was closer than the office. I knew there was a sink in there, and my mom headed behind the counter as I stood with Frankie and Wyatt just outside the door. The girl behind the counter looked from my mom, to us, and back to my mom.

I started to open my mouth to explain but closed it again without saying a word. I just stood there patting Wyatt on the head hoping he'd quiet down so no one would notice us.

As my mom leaned over the sink trying to control the bleeding, the counter-girl rushed out. I assumed she was either going to get help or running for her life. Either way, she wasn't here witnessing this humiliation, which was okay by me.

"...TOMORROW AFTERNOON. YEAH. IT'S A KID'S BIRTHDAY PARTY."

Someone was approaching the counter talking quietly on a cell phone. I tried to shush Wyatt in case it was someone I knew. Through napkins and paper towels covering her face, my mom replied, "You'll have to wait a minute. Someone will be right with you."

I peeked around the corner where the three of us were standing to see if I recognized the voice on the phone. It seemed familiar, I just couldn't place it. As I peered around the corner, the young man turned toward me. Holy crap! It was Mark Lerner. I recognized him from the neighborhood. He was a couple of years older, but easily the cutest boy I'd ever seen. I couldn't risk being seen here. Not with my little brother wailing, and my mom covered in blood. What would he think? My teen years would be ruined! My mind reeled, and as I grabbed Wyatt and ducked back around the corner, I put my hand over his mouth. This only served to make him cry harder.

Mark's voice was getting louder, and I was starting to panic, looking for someplace to hide. I saw a stack of boxes a short distance away and made my decision. "Sorry, Wyatt, you're on your own." He looked confused when I dropped his hand, took two steps, put my arm in the rolling position I'd been taught and did a perfect front roll with a breakfall! My parents would be so proud. Except for the part about abandoning Wyatt while he was crying, I guessed.

While Mark talked, he appeared to be pushing a broom in the general direction of the basketball courts.

"...I said tomorrow!" He finally concluded his call and hung up abruptly continuing to push the broom toward the courts without noticing any of us. Fortunately.

"That was a relief," I said, coming out from behind the boxes. "I'm not really sure how to work a cash register." I looked sheepishly at my mom, hoping she didn't notice that I had temporarily left my post as big sister. My mom's gaze followed Mark.

"Who was that?" she asked.

"Uh, I think it was one of the janitors. He was pushing a broom...kind of. He was talking about a birthday party here tomorrow, so I guess he works here?"

"Oh." Not really listening to the answer, she said, "Alright, get your stuff. I've had enough fun for one day. Let's go home."

"AWW. MOM!" ALL THREE OF US GROANED IN UNISON.

"Are you kidding me?!" She looked at us, her one good eye opened wide. "Not sure if you noticed, but I'm pretty sure my nose is broken." We looked at her swollen nose, her already blackening eyes, and briefly exchanged a look of guilt.

"Um, mom?" I asked. Feeling slightly guilty, but still wanting to do some sleuthing. She looked at me expectantly. "Not to take away from the personal crisis you're having here, but is it okay if I walk home?" The club was only about a mile from our house, and I'd walked it before. And it was the middle of the day after all.

"Why?" she asked.

"Well, I thought I'd hang around and find Mrs. Marlin?"

"Fine." She must have really been feeling bad, because she would normally argue with me, especially after this morning. Apparently, getting hit in the face with a tennis racket took her mind off how mad she was at me. As it was, she just said, "Don't be late, and be careful."

"Hmmm," I thought, "maybe her injury is a good thing." Then I looked at her. Nope. Definitely not.

Frankie and I exchanged horrified looks. Our mom had gotten some bruises out in the dojo, but she never looked this bad before. Maybe she should stick to martial arts training. At the moment, it seemed safer.

CHAPTER TWELVE

My mom met Mrs. Marlin at the tennis club about a year ago and they'd become fast friends. We called her Mrs. M because she always said being called Mrs. Marlin made her feel like a fish. I looked it up once and it turns out a marlin is a pretty big fish. She didn't look like a fish though. She was blond and pretty and about the same height as my mom. She was a bit of a tomboy like my mom, so they got along great and found out they had a lot in common, not the least of which was that their love of tennis and lack of skill was about the same. Mrs. M's husband was a high-level executive at a local software company and, according to my mom, kept her in the lap of luxury.

My mom once pointed out the size of Mrs. M's engagement ring when we were at the tennis club. "How is that woman going to play if she has to lug that thing around on her hand all day?" she said to me under her breath as she looked down at her own modest ring.

As if reading my mom's mind, Mrs. M had answered the question, "I know. Hideous, isn't it?" She held out the ring and looked at it with a look that was almost embarrassment. "I'm not sure why he had to buy one this big; I was just as happy with a small one, like yours." She stopped, realizing what she'd said. "I didn't mean...er...uh..." she trailed off.

"No problem," my mom had answered. "I know what you mean."

"Yeah, I take it off when I'm playing tennis. Sometimes other women are so distracted by it; they can't seem to concentrate." She looked up. "You'd think that would be a good thing, and I would win more matches, but it's easier just to take it off." Changing the subject, she got up abruptly, put her ring in her purse which she promptly locked up in her locker, grabbed her tennis racket, and headed out to the courts without another word. They were friends from that moment on.

I thought about that as I rounded the corner and saw Mrs. M stow her ring in her purse and put it into her locker.

"Hey, Mrs. M," I called.

"Hey Sam, where's your mom?"

"Uh, she was here but she had to get Frankie and Wyatt home," I paused wondering if I should give her the gory details but decided against it. "So, my mom told me that your ring was stolen?"

"That's right," she said, "Why?" She had a weird look on her face.

"Not sure if my mom told you, but I'm opening up my own detective agency, and I thought you could use my help." I paused when she looked amused but kept on going. "I already solved my first case, you know. I helped the Batemans get their dog back!"

She swallowed her amusement, and said, "You're hired! I hope you're not too expensive. What do you want to know?"

"Since I'm just starting out, this will be no charge," I said seriously, "But just because you're friends with my mom." I looked down at the bag I was carrying and didn't notice Mrs. M put her hand over her mouth to hide a smile. I had a notebook in my bag labeled "Sam's Case Notes" not to be confused with "Sam's Martial Arts Notes" which I also liked to carry around. It made me feel more official. "So, you took it in to be cleaned. Then what?" I poised my pencil over my notepad in case she said anything I needed to investigate later.

"I took it to the same jeweler I've been taking it to since I got it, and he said it's a fake! He said this is not the same ring that I've been bringing in for the last ten years. So, I'm not sure if one of his other helpers replaced the diamond, or what. But the police are looking into it."

"They are?" I wondered if my dad is working on this case? "Did they say anything?" I tried to sound nonchalant.

"They're looking into the backgrounds of all the people who work in the jewelry store, but I don't think it was them. We've known them too long." She sounded dejected. "And, they're the ones who told me it was a fake. So, I don't think they'd do that if they're the ones who stole it, right?"

"Probably not," I agreed. "Well, thanks Mrs. M. I'll start to look into this for you."

She smiled again and had that amused look on her face. "Ask your mom when she wants to play tennis again, okay? Tell her any day but

Saturday. I have a tennis lesson in the morning, and then I'm having my son's birthday party in the afternoon. I rented one of those rooms they have here at the club, instead of having all of his friends make a mess of my house! I thought I'd let someone else clean up for a change. They give all the kids a tennis lesson, feed them, and even throw in a magician for good measure! I was at another kid's birthday party here a couple of months ago and the kids seemed to have a blast. Hopefully, it'll be fun."

"I'll ask her and have her call you," I promised, wondering if she would be playing tennis any time soon.

CHAPTER THIRTEEN

"What happens if you get hit in the face again?" I asked.

"Do you really think Mrs. Marlin is going to whack me in the face with a tennis racket?"

"No, I meant with a ball."

"YOU THINK SHE'S GOING TO WHACK ME IN THE FACE WITH A BALL? WHY WOULD SHE DO THAT?"

"No. I mean if you miss and it just hits you in the face?"

"How bad would I have to be to get hit in the face with a tennis ball, while I was actually playing tennis? I'm not that bad, you know." She had her hands on her hips now, waiting for my response.

"Uh, ok. If you say so." I let it drop. Of course, she was that uncoordinated. How did she think she got hit in the first place? It's not like she had the reflexes of a cat. But whatever. "So, I think I'll go to my room and start googling fake jewelry to see what I can find out. If I'm going to think like a thief, I better learn as much as I can about diamonds, jewelers, and the fake jewelry biz as I can; don't you think?" Wanting as much to be done with this conversation as to start my investigation, I exited the room before she could argue with me.

CHAPTER FOURTEEN

My dad had left that morning by way of the dojo and when he returned home, he came in the same way.

He usually liked to get to work early on days that he had to teach a class but being a detective for the local police department could be kind of demanding. I know he'd been working on some major theft cases in the area, since table talk at dinner tended to revolve around his job. He occasionally left the files out on the counter, and recently the top files had to do with missing or stolen jewelry. He also tended to talk to himself when he was trying to find a link in some cases.

When he finally walked back in through the doorway that night, eight kids had already shown up to class, and Frankie and I had taken our place in line. His eyebrows raised in surprise seeing us in line. Usually we were late because we were trying to stall, but now that I'd actually had the chance to use one of the techniques we learned in class I was more anxious than usual to learn other techniques that might come in handy. Today for the first time in a long time, I was eager to learn.

"OKAY, PAIR OFF IN TWOS AND LINE UP IN THE MIDDLE OF THE FLOOR," MY MOM SHOUTED.

"Shite" (pronounced Shhh-tay) she said pointing to the girls on the right, "is the girl doing the technique. Uke" (pronounced ooo-kay) she said pointing to the girls on the left, "is the girl receiving the technique. Shites, you have a choice today. You can either do Morote Seoi Nage" (pronounced Ma-row-tay Say-oy Nah-gay). She waited for any glimmer of understanding, and when she got none, she continued, "Or you can do Tomoe Nage"[2] (pronounced Toe-muh Nah-gay). She waited again. "Anyone?" All the girls lined up were careful not to make eye contact.

I exchanged glances with the other girls. We were supposed to know the techniques by their Japanese names but learning them in English was hard enough. Finally, after ten or fifteen agonizing seconds, she told us, in English, what we should be doing. "Throwing techniques, girls. You have the choice of your two-handed throw; this would be Morote Seoi Nage," she said it slowly, pronouncing every syllable. "Or you can do the stomach throw, Tomoe Nage."

"Hmmmm," I thought to myself. "I can either pick Catherine up and hoist her over my shoulder," I cringed inwardly, "or I can lay on ground and use my feet to throw her." Catherine was about my size and thin, but if there's a laying on the ground option, I'll take it every time.

2

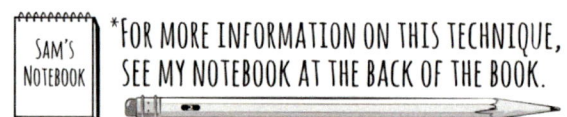

*FOR MORE INFORMATION ON THIS TECHNIQUE, SEE MY NOTEBOOK AT THE BACK OF THE BOOK.

"Tomoe Nage it is!"

My dad smiled as he finally went into the house. Compared to catching criminals all day, I'm sure this was the best part of his day. Not always the best part of mine, but at least it made someone happy.

As he was standing there, he glanced at my mom, and his eyes grew wide and he gasped loudly. I think she forgot for a moment how bad she looked, until she saw his face. She waved her hand at him as if to indicate it was nothing, but he just stood there staring. I'm sure he was wondering if one of the kids in her class accidentally punched her in the face, but he didn't want to interrupt her teaching to ask her.

CHAPTER FIFTEEN

"So, what was the date of the cleaning?" I asked. I'd gotten enough information from Mrs. Marlin to begin doing some research on her missing ring.

He hesitated. "Who is this again?"

"I'm the insurance adjuster," saying the first thing that came into my head. "I just have a few simple questions." I held my breath waiting for him to hang up on me.

"You sound kind of young," he hesitated.

"Yeah, I get that a lot," I replied. "What was the date again?" I held my breath.

He hesitated for a second but answered the question. "She had it cleaned on March 10th. Why?"

"Just need it for the insurance claim," I said, trying to sound official. "And, what made you first think that the diamond she gave you to clean was fake?" I was speaking to the owner of B&L Jewels, where Mrs. Marlin had originally purchased her diamond and had it cleaned on a fairly regular basis and tried to use my most grown-up voice.

"WELL, FIRST OFF, IT WAS TOO PERFECT."

"Uh...and that's a bad thing...?" I asked.

"Of course," the owner of B&L Jewels, Mr. Langley, said in disbelief. "Real diamonds have flaws, tiny mistakes. They may not be perfectly shaped. A cubic zirconium, however, is perfectly shaped because it can be carefully crafted." I could practically hear him shaking his head at my ignorance of jewelry. Obviously, this was elementary knowledge that everyone should possess.

"Oh. Anything else?" I asked.

"Well, it was missing the certification number. They have come up with a machine that will inscribe a hologram under the table facet that can be seen with a special viewer. Laser-inscribed diamonds place a diamond certificate number or some other identifying feature on the diamond. The laser-inscribed mark is extremely small and requires a jeweler's loupe to view the laser-inscribed diamond mark."

I WAS WRITING FURIOUSLY. THIS WAS ALL NEW INFORMATION.

"Our thief was not counting on his victim to be so dedicated to having her diamond cleaned. If she hadn't brought it in to me, her regular jeweler, this theft might not have been detected for a very long time. Not all jewelers are as sophisticated as we are to have the certificate numbers engraved." He was almost smug by the time he finished.

"Thanks for your cooperation, Mr. Langley. If we need anything else, we'll be in touch." I hung up before he could ask me any questions about insurance.

I didn't really suspect the jeweler of being in on it, especially since he was the one who notified the police department in the first place, so I checked him off my list of suspects. It was a short list, since I wasn't quite sure where to begin. I was surprised at the value of the ring, however, noting that the street value was approximately $25,000, which is why she was so fussy about having it cleaned. She took it in about every six months, so in theory all I had to do is trace her steps over the last couple of months and I should be able to figure out what happened. How hard could it be?

CHAPTER SIXTEEN

In addition to talking to Mrs. M's jeweler, I had been busily research-ing diamonds for the last couple of hours. Apparently, there are the five "Cs" of buying a diamond. Cut, Clarity, Color, Carat, and Cost! And, in your more expensive diamonds, they engrave an identifying mark on the underside somewhere.

I went into the living room to run some theories by my mom. "Her ring was pretty big, right?"

"Uh, yeah...big is an understatement." My mom shook her head, glancing down at her own tiny ring. "I wonder what a ring like that cost," she wondered out loud.

"IT HAS A STREET VALUE OF $25, 000," I ANSWERED TOO QUICKLY

"What?! How do you know that?" She looked at me curiously.

"Research," I muttered, "So in a town like this, where could someone sell something like that?"

"Not sure," my mom responded, "I guess I hadn't thought about it."

"My guess is the internet," I said. "You know, eBay, Craigslist, cash-4gold.com. Sites like that. So, all we need is a picture of Mrs. M's ring, and we can do a reverse image search online!"

My mom sat there for a moment mulling over what I had just said, not sure whether to be proud or skeptical. "Hold on." She grabbed her phone. "I have a picture of the two of us winning that doubles trophy last year. I think I might actually have a picture of her ring." She skimmed through the pictures on her phone quickly. "Here it is. Will this work?"

"I thought you said she took off her ring when you played," I won-dered out loud.

"Yes, but pictures were being taken, so she fixed her hair and makeup and put back on her ring." She smiled. "You know how us girls do."

I smiled back at her. Us tomboys had to stick together. It was okay not to fix your hair and makeup for pictures, but not all girls seemed to know that. I looked back at the photo.

I tried to enlarge the picture of them holding the trophy together to get a better view of her ring. "Well, it's a little blurry when you enlarge it, but not terrible. Maybe we could get a better one?"

"Ok," my mom said, "Maybe we'll drop in on her birthday party on Saturday? In the meantime, maybe we can get more information out of your dad. I'm pretty sure he's been assigned the case. He hasn't said so, but the way he clammed up when I started talking about it, was a sure sign."

Usually, if my dad was uninvolved in a case, or if it was something they saw on TV, he would speculate with my mom, and sometimes me, about the possible motives and solutions. But anytime he was directly involved with something, he clammed up tighter than a drum, so as not to inadvertently slip with confidential information. Last night when my mom was talking about her phone conversation with Mrs. M, he hadn't said a word. Maybe my mom was right.

CHAPTER SEVENTEEN

"Well, where do you think she is," I asked my mom, "And what are we going to do with these kids?" I gestured to Frankie and Wyatt.

My mom rolled her eyes at me, but said, "I'm not sure my nose can take any more tennis lessons, so you go look for her; I'll find a game for these two to play, then I'll come find you. And, if Mrs. M is playing tennis before her party, she's probably down at the courts."

"C'mon, you guys," my mom called. They headed off in the direction of the basketball courts. "You hold my purse," she said handing me her ginormous bag, "I'll get them started on a game."

I checked out the courts and Mrs. M wasn't there, so I went to the front desk to find out which room she had the birthday party scheduled for. "Last name is Marlin," I told the girl behind the counter. "She reserved a room to have a birthday party for her son, Austin. Can you tell me which room it is?" I waited while the girl looked through a big binder of event listings.

I looked around as I stood there. It was a small office with a front counter just inside the main entrance. There were usually kids employed at the front desk who either doubled as lifeguards or tennis instructors, but had to pull a certain number of hours doing clerical work as well. Off to the right were the tennis courts and the girls' locker rooms, and off to the left were the weight rooms and the boys' locker rooms. The swimming pool was on the way to the tennis courts, and event rooms were on both sides.

The girl looking through the binder couldn't find what she was looking for and called one of the coaches over to help. His name tag said Coach Mike. He was about six feet tall with short brown hair. He was in his late teens I guessed and judging by the way the girls behind the counter were looking at him he must have been considered cute. You know, for an old guy. His hair was cut in a military style and he looked like he worked out. The girl who called him stopped looking through the book and just gazed at him while he tried to find the information. Ugh, if that's what being a teenager was all about, I wanted no part of it.

Instead of watching her watch him, I rummaged through my mom's purse for a stick of gum. Her purse seemed to be a collection of odd items. I'm sure she had gum in there somewhere, but I had to pull out a number of items just to get to it. I put her phone on the counter, followed by her keys, a shopping list, Wyatt's whistle, a toy car, Frankie's necklace that she'd been in search of for about a week, a flashlight, a balloon, and finally, gum! As I pulled out these items, crumbs from what must have been a left-over cookie fell to the floor. I looked up in time to catch the eye of a young man who'd been sweeping the floors. He glared at me as the crumbs fell to his nice clean floor. Quickly, I grabbed an old crumpled up Kleenex, that had also been in her purse (I hoped it hadn't been used) and wiped up as many crumbs as I could. Then, of course, I shoved everything back into her purse.

The counter girl finally found what she was looking for. "Here's the room number," she said and handed me the piece of paper.

"Thanks," I said and started walking off down the hallway toward the party rooms. Within a couple of minutes, I arrived at the Mensa Room. "Weird name for a party room," I thought. "Hi there," I said to Mrs. Marlin, who looked pretty frazzled for a woman who'd planned a party away from her house in an effort to reduce stress. "How's it going?"

She looked momentarily confused when she saw me but said "I'm glad you're here." She sounded relieved and didn't even question what I was doing there.

"You are?"

"Yeah. None of the parents stayed to help, like they usually do at my house. So even though they aren't in my dining room, fifteen boys are still a lot of boys."

NOT KNOWING WHAT ELSE TO SAY, I SAID, "HOW CAN I HELP?"

"You have a loud voice, right, from all that karate? Can you just get them all to sit over there?" she pointed to a cleared space over on the side of the room. "The magician is about to start."

"Uh, ok." Not sure how my taking karate gave me a loud voice, but this didn't seem like the time to argue. I just rolled up my sleeves. Any thoughts about questioning Mrs. M about her missing diamond were temporarily gone from my head. This was nearly at crisis level, and if there was one thing I could spot a mile away, it was a woman on the verge of a nervous breakdown. For the good of everyone involved, I knew I had better help out.

"Line up!" I bellowed at the top of my voice. Startled, they stopped. They didn't exactly line up, but they did stop talking long enough to look around to see who was yelling. Once I had their attention I yelled again. "Alright, the magician is about to start, so if any of you even think you're going to have cake or ice cream, get your butts over on the floor in that corner over there, and give him a nice round of applause."

Mrs. M looked impressed. She'd been dealing with the screaming kids for the last hour and a half by herself. Except for an occasional helper appearing to clean up plates, and the tennis lesson not lasting nearly long enough, they didn't have enough activities to distract them. She opened the door for the magician and was surprised to see Coach Mike, the same man that just taught the kids tennis, and had just helped me at the front desk.

"ARE YOU THE MAGICIAN, TOO?"

She hoped the shock didn't appear in her voice.

"Yep." He seemed used to this reaction. "Hey kids, how would you like to see some magic?" The boys seemed used to listening to him for instruction, so they were reasonably attentive.

"Yeah!" they cried in unison.

"Ok, sit back and enjoy the show! So, where's the birthday boy?" Coach Mike asked.

The boys all pointed to Austin who looked slightly embarrassed.

"How old are you, Austin?"

"I'm eight."

For the next hour, Coach Mike, or Magic Mike as he was sometimes referred to by the girls in the club, performed cursory magic tricks. A few card tricks, some interlocking ring tricks, disappearing coins, etc. I could tell the show was coming to a close, and so far, I was pretty unimpressed.

"Now for my grand finale," he said, "I'll make something in the room disappear. What shall it be?" he asked the boys.

"Make Mrs. Marlin disappear!" one of the boys yelled.

"Yeah, make my mom disappear," yelled Austin.

"Well, I didn't bring my big box this time," he looked at Mrs. M who was looking nervous. "How about if we make something she's wearing disappear?"

"How about her ring?"

The boys agreed once they saw the size of the diamond. Not knowing it was only zirconium at this point, they clapped praying that something would go horribly wrong.

AT THE MENTION OF HER RING, I BECAME MORE INTERESTED. MY ATTENTION WAS ON THE MAGICIAN.

"May I?" he asked Mrs. Marlin.

"Not again," she said under her breath. Then willingly, she gave up her ring.

All the boys sat forward as Magic Mike asked for Mrs. Marlin's ring. He showed the boys the ring before placing it into a handkerchief. He carefully folded the ring inside the handkerchief and handed it to Mrs. Marlin.

"Hang on to this and don't let go," he warned. He spent the next several moments going through his magician speak and delivered some not-so-bad jokes. Finally, when every moment of anticipation had been exhausted and the crowd was nearing boredom, he pulled a folded key ring out of his pocket. He held it up for the crowd to see. Without saying another word but making a great show of the key holder, he opened the folded leather item. Inside the snapped, folded key ring was Carrie's ring, hanging on a clasp.

The boys, as well as Mrs. M and I were stunned and impressed.

"How did he do that?" they began asking each other. While the boys were joking, Magic Mike—he had now earned the title—put the key ring into his pocket.

Mrs. M held out her hand.

"Oh, yeah," he feigned embarrassment. "I guess this is yours." He took the ring off the hook and handed it back to her.

"Pretty good trick," Mrs. M said more to herself than to me, but I was lost in thought.

"C'mon boys, your moms will be here soon. Get your goody bags and start gathering your stuff." Finally, the party was over. I said goodbye to Mrs. M and hurried off to go find my mom to tell her what I'd discovered. I had more theories to explore.

CHAPTER EIGHTEEN

I hurried to the courts to find my mom.

"How'd it go?" My mom glanced at her watch. "I was going to come and find you, but..." her voice trailed off as she looked at Frankie and Wyatt. "So, what did you find out?"

"I got sucked into being a helper at the party," I complained. "I was babysitting fifteen kids and didn't even get paid."

A basketball whacked my mom in the back of the head as she listened to my complaint. Without even turning around she said, "Would you rather have been here?"

I LOOKED TO WHERE FRANKIE AND WYATT WERE GIGGLING AT MY MOM'S LATEST INJURY. "I GUESS NOT."

"Get your stuff and let's go. You can tell me all about it on the way to lunch. I told your Aunt Sharon we'd meet her for lunch. I better call her to tell her we'll be late." She started to rummage through her purse to look for her phone. "What the....?" Her voice trailed off. She knelt down on the court and dumped out her purse. We watched in amazement.

"What's all that stuff," Wyatt asked. He bent down to pick up his car that rolled out of his mom's purse. "This is mine," he said accusingly, "Why do you have it?"

My mom didn't bother to answer. She was frantically trying to remember where she'd last seen her phone.

"Um," I cleared my throat. "I may or may not have gone through your purse looking for gum. And may or may not have put your phone on the counter at the front desk. And there's the remote possibility that I forgot to put it back in your purse."

"And...?" my mom said looking annoyed.

"Why don't I go check for you?" I hurried toward the front desk. I approached, but no one was there. As I stood there waiting, I looked over the counter and saw my mom's phone sitting right where I left it. I grabbed it up and ran back to the car before anyone came back.

"Here you go," I handed it to my mom as if nothing had happened.

She glared at me as she pushed the number 1, which was the speed dial number for her sister.

"Hello," a male voice said.

"Hello? Who is this?" My mom looked confused. She had been expecting her sister's voice and was taken aback when a man answered.

"Bob. Who's this?"

"Jane. Is Sharon there?"

"Sorry, you must have the wrong number."

"Did I dial 248 555 6143?"

"Nope. Sorry." The voice was starting to sound impatient.

"Sorry to have bothered you." My mom hung up the phone and just stared at it. The number was pre-programmed, so how could it be wrong. What the heck? She decided to check the number that she had programmed in. She hit the word "contact" on the phone, and pushed the letter S. "Why can't I find her name in here?" Now she was thoroughly confused. As she sat there, she thought, "And why is my screensaver different?" It finally dawned on her. "This isn't my phone," she said to me.

"Huh? It sure looks like your phone," I said. "It has pictures like your phone."

"Where did you get it?" she asked.

"At the front desk where I left it. I had to reach over the counter, because no one was there, but it was lying on the counter. I just assumed it was yours."

"Obviously not." Without a word she handed me the phone. I got out of the car and ran back to the counter to see whose phone I had actually taken.

CHAPTER NINETEEN

I managed to retrieve her phone from the janitor who was standing at the counter looking as confused as my mom had, staring at her phone in his hand.

"Hey there," I said running up to him, "I think I grabbed your phone by accident." He looked more nervous than angry when I handed it back to him. "My mom tried to make a call, but her sister is not programmed into your phone," I tried to make a joke. "She talked to somebody named Bob instead." I smiled. He snatched the phone out of my hand and quickly threw me my mom's phone. He looked a little scared when I mentioned Bob and his phone began to ring as he turned away.

"Yeah, I know Bob," he said. "It was a mix-up with the phones."

I WATCHED AFTER HIM FOR A SECOND BUT WAS RELIEVED TO HAVE MY MOM'S PHONE BACK AND RUSHED BACK TO THE CAR WHERE SHE WAS WAITING.

"...okay, see you later," my mom hung up the phone.

"Really, he made her ring disappear." I was trying to explain the magic trick to my mom. "I don't think he could have stolen it right then, because he would have had to have an exact replica on him to replace it. But right before he took her ring from her, she said something like 'not again.' Maybe that means he's used her ring for this trick before?" I looked at her hopefully.

"You know," my mom smiled, "I think you might be on to something. Now, all we have to do is find out if she's been at a kid's birthday party before this one. Nice work, Sam! You actually have a knack for this detective thing," she paused, "You just need to be more careful."

Hmmm. A compliment mixed in with a warning. Another parental trick used to render a kid speechless. And it was working. Not sure which part of her statement to react to, I went with the former, and not the latter.

"Thanks, so how do we do that?" Ignoring her statement about being careful, I was already developing a devious plot that would involve sneaking around at the tennis club at night with flashlights, and maybe a grappling hook and some rope. This could be fun.

"How about asking her? Doesn't that sound like a logical place to start?"

"Oh," I said, clearly disappointed. Her and her logic. I'm 12. I don't want logic. I want fun, excitement, danger even. Well, maybe not danger. I'm kind of a scaredy cat, after all. But fun and excitement at least. "Call her? Really? That's it? After all I went through?"

"WENT THROUGH? YOU MEAN A PARTY? CAKE? ICE CREAM? A MAGIC SHOW? POOR YOU. I'M NOT SURE HOW YOU'VE RECOVERED FROM ALL THAT MAYHEM."

"Let's call her and ask her then," I said, hiding my disappointment.

My dad walked into the room reading a file. He looked back and forth between the two of us, not quite knowing what was going on. "What are you doing," he said to my mom.

"I'm calling Mrs. M," she said without further explanation, and he continued to read his file.

"Hi Carrie," she said. "Sam said it was a great party today. How are you recovering?" She paused to let her friend talk. "So, that magician was pretty good?" I was paying attention now. "So, Sam heard you say, 'not again,'" she said trying to sound casual, "has he done this trick before?"

Now I was standing right next to my mom trying to hear Mrs. M's response. My mom pulled the phone away from her ear, so I could hear too.

"Yeah, as a matter of fact," Mrs. M said, "I was at a birthday party for a friend of Austin's a couple of months ago, the Patterson boy, do you know him?" Without waiting for a response, she continued, "...and he did the same trick then." She laughed a bit self-consciously. "I guess this thing is so big; it's kind of an easy target. Why do you ask?"

"No reason," my mom replied. "Just curious. So how are you otherwise?" My mom wanted to change the subject so as not to arouse Mrs. M's suspicions.

I went and sat on the couch next to my dad while my mom finished her call.

"AH, HAH!" MY MOM ENTERED THE ROOM, TRIUMPHANT.

"What?" my dad was oblivious to anything that had been going on.

"She was at a birthday party before and had the same trick done to her at that one," she paused, "Sam might be on to something."

"What have you two been up to now?" His tone was accusatory. Not the proud moment that I was anticipating.

"Well," I began. "We just happened to be at the tennis club today…"

"Just happened to be?" he interrupted.

I explained my theory to him and added the story of the magic trick at the birthday party and concluded with the results of the phone call. "So, what do you think?"

"Hmmm. Did you ask her the date of the first party?"

"No, why?"

"Well, how do you know it didn't happen after her ring had already been switched."

"Uh…"

"Don't you think maybe we have a couple more details to flesh out before you go awarding yourself the key to the city?"

"Well, I can just call the club and find out when the party was. Then we'll know for sure if it was before or after her ring had been switched." My theory must have some merit, or he would have just grunted and gone back to reading his file. But he'd actually put it down and listened. I guess I had a knack for this detective thing after all.

CHAPTER TWENTY

"When do you think it was?" the girl on the phone asked.

"Sometime in March?" I suggested.

"Hmmmm...well, I don't see any...oh, yeah, here it is. March 7th."

"Great! Thanks, that's all I needed." I hung up the phone, smiling. "Yes!" I went to high-five my mom, but it must not have seemed high-five-worthy so she just stared at me.

"What?" she asked.

"The Pattersons had a birthday party on March 7th!" I said excitedly.

"OH, WELL IN THAT CASE. WOO HOO! HIGH FIVE, SAM!"

She put her hand up in the air in mock excitement. "So?" she was confused.

"Don't you see?" I said.

"Obviously not. Feel free to clarify."

"Well that means, if Mrs. M went to the Pattersons' birthday party on March 7th, but she had her ring cleaned on March 10th, it could have been switched at that party."

CHAPTER TWENTY-ONE

"Owww," I groaned as I hit the mat for what seemed like the millionth time. "Oomph." I hit the ground hard this time. Supposedly, these would get easier with time and practice, but I'd seen no evidence of that so far.

"Matte" (pronounced Mah-tay). This is the most important word to learn in the martial arts because it meant "Stop." Immediately. It either meant you got to rest, or that someone would stop hurting you. Both were good. My dad was leading class tonight.

"Now that you're all warmed up," he said, "Zenpo Kaiten Ukemi"[3] (pronounced zen-poe kie-ten ooo-kay-mee).

SAM'S NOTEBOOK

*FOR MORE INFORMATION ON THIS TECHNIQUE, SEE MY NOTEBOOK AT THE BACK OF THE BOOK.

3

I looked at my mom who was working out in the same class with me. She smiled at me. She wasn't used to seeing me in so many classes so was hoping that I continued to enjoy it.

I watched while my dad performed the technique that he wanted us to execute. This was one technique I knew I could do, thinking back to the roll I'd executed at the Tennis Club. Rolls were something they started teaching students on day one, so adding a breakfall didn't seem that difficult.

"Well, no time like the present, right?" Catherine, my training partner, launched into perfect roll and stopped herself with a breakfall like she'd been doing it her whole life.

I followed her lead, took a step, reached out with my right arm, bent over, kept my arm stiff, and kicked my left leg over. I did a perfect roll with a perfect breakfall at the end. I looked at Catherine who looked mildly impressed. "Nice job, Sam," she said.

"RIGHT BACK AT YA, PARTNER," I RETURNED THE COMPLIMENT.

After rolls were over, we began to work on our basic techniques. Ever since the run-in with our dognapping neighbor, I'd been training a little harder. If one technique worked, maybe there was some other stuff I could learn as well.

I got Catherine in the mount, a basic jujitsu position, and waited while she readied herself. She bent her knees, protected her head with her elbows and waited for me to execute the technique I wanted to work on. When I applied just the right amount of pressure, she tapped out, indicating I should stop. Tapping out[4] was almost as important as the word "Matte." And it meant the same thing. Stop. Immediately. As my dad always said, "There's a fine line between hurt and broken. Don't cross it." So, my personal mantra was "tap early, tap often." You know, just to be safe.

4

SAM'S NOTEBOOK *FOR MORE INFORMATION ON THIS TECHNIQUE, SEE MY NOTEBOOK AT THE BACK OF THE BOOK.

I tried to execute the techniques like I'd seen my dad do. I managed to finish without too much trouble. Maybe I was a chip off the old block after all. I switched positions with Catherine and let her try the techniques she wanted to work on. We went back and forth for the next hour and a half.

Finally, it was over. Dripping with sweat, I glanced around. "Well, that went pretty fast," I thought, "And, it was actually kind of fun."

YIKES. WAS I ACTUALLY BEGINNING TO LIKE IT? BETTER KEEP THAT TO MYSELF, OR MY PARENTS MIGHT GET IDEAS.

CHAPTER TWENTY-TWO

"Good class," my mom said to my dad when we all finally got back into the house.

"Yeah, they all seemed to like it," he replied.

"Yeah, it was fun," I added. They both stopped and looked at me. "What?" I said. "Can't a girl enjoy a good workout, without getting weird looks from her parents?" I opened the refrigerator looking for a water bottle.

"Uh…" They were both speechless. This was good. Maybe I should enjoy working out more often.

"Who are you, and what did you do with Samantha," my dad finally managed to say.

I rolled my eyes. "There she is," my mom said. "There's the Sam I know and love. I didn't recognize her at first without the eye rolling. Now if you could just talk to us like we're idiots, we'll know it's you for sure."

"UGH, MOM," I ROLLED MY EYES AGAIN FOR AFFECT, MUTTERED "WHATEVER" UNDER MY BREATH, AND LEFT THE ROOM.

"Yes, identification is complete," she said. She shook her head, got a glass of water, and followed me into the living room.

"So," my dad started, "You know I'm working on some other theft cases in the city involving high-price items, right?"

I stopped in mid-gulp and just looked at my dad. Usually he didn't divulge information about his cases, so this was unusual. "Uh, of course," I said, but was thinking, "How would I know that?"

"In fact," he said, "Of the six cases, all of the victims belong to the Tennis Club, and four had birthday parties scheduled that involved the magician, and the other two didn't know."

"Didn't know?" I said. "They didn't know if their own kid had a birthday party or not, or they didn't know if they had a magician?" I was confused.

"I talked to the dads," he started.

"Oh, the dads," my mom and I exchanged knowing glances. We women knew things.

He paused. He hated when we teamed up. "I'll track down the wives tomorrow," he said. "It's kind of late now." We all glanced at the clock. It was nearly 10 p.m. "And, the last one, Mrs. Wagner, said for sure they didn't belong to the club."

"Mrs. Wagner?" I said, "Is that Emily's mom?"

They both looked at me. "Emily?" my mom said.

"Yeah, she's the girl in Frankie's Girl Scout troop who has the iPhone." My mom was staring at me.

"I remember that now," she said, "Frankie came home and talked about this really cool phone. I think they surfed the net while they were at that meeting. Remember? Frankie asked if she could have one too, and we both laughed hysterically."

"Now that you mention it," my dad said, "I do remember that."

"Well, it would fit, wouldn't it?"

"What?"

"WELL, IF THE 9-YEAR-OLD HAS AN IPHONE, THEN IT STANDS TO REASON SHE WOULD HAVE A MOM WITH AN EXPENSIVE PIECE OF JEWELRY?"

"And," I added excitedly, "They earned that badge back in February at the club, where they had to do tennis and swimming, and one other thing, I think. The magician is also the tennis coach. The Wagners are members, right? You just said so. Maybe she was at this event too?"

"That's a lot of maybes," he said, but was starting to admit the possibility.

"Well?"

"What?"

"Aren't you going to call her?"

"Not right now, it's too late." He pointed to the clock.

"Well, let's at least ask Frankie. She was at that event; maybe she'll remember something." We all hurried into the living room, where Frankie was curled up in a chair reading one of the *Harry Potter* books, again. My dad glanced at the clock. "Don't these kids ever go to bed?" he said to my mom as they approached their daughter.

"We're homeschooled, remember? We don't need to get up at the crack of dawn, so they don't need to go to bed early. And, anyway, if they did, you'd never see them."

He had to admit that this last part was true. "Hey, Frankie," he scooped her up and put himself where she had been. Now she was sitting on his lap wondering what had just happened.

"What, Dad?" she asked.

"Remember when you were at the Tennis Club a long time ago, and you earned a badge for doing tennis and swimming?"

"Yeah," she said, "I remember."

"GREAT," HE SAID. "TELL ME EVERYTHING YOU REMEMBER ABOUT IT."

He let her go first so he wouldn't plant any ideas.

"Well, I remember playing tennis," she said looking at both parents and me wondering why they were both so interested in something that happened so long ago. "The day we got to go swimming it was really cold." She shivered recalling it. For some unknown reason she was the center of attention, but she kept going. "Then we had something to eat, and then we danced." She stopped, proud that she recalled all of these details.

"Danced?" Mom prompted.

"Yeah, we had to do three things for the badge," she said, "And dancing was the third thing."

"Do you remember anything else?" Dad asked gently.

"Uh, like what?" Frankie wasn't exactly sure what they were looking for.

"Like who was there for example?"

"Uh, well the girls in my troop."

"Did they all come?"

"Yep, I think so."

"What were their names, do you remember?" Mom asked.

"Of course I do!" She turned away from Mom and looked at Dad.

"Can you tell me who they were?"

"Sure. Andrea, Erin, Maggie, Natalie, Tessa, Anna, Elayna, and Emily." She looked at Dad for praise.

"Hmmm, the plot thickens," I said.

"Anything else?" Dad asked.

"Well," she paused. "There was a pretty cool magic show." She didn't notice that both her parents and her big sister were now riveted to every word. "I remember because it was pretty lame when it first started. You know, he did the usual stuff. He pulled a coin out of Andrea's nose." She giggled. "That was actually kind of funny. Then he made Emily's mom's watch disappear. It was really cool. I remember she got really nervous and started talking about how expensive it was. She was almost freaking out."

"Thanks, kiddo." Dad patted her on the head one more time and set her back in the chair to continue reading.

"So," I said to Dad, "That's too many to be a coincidence and they've all been to a party at the club in the last six months. Guess I'll go back there tomorrow and finish my investigating." I turned and walked to my room while they stared after me.

CHAPTER TWENTY-THREE

"Hey, Dad. Whatcha doin?" I bounded down first thing in the morning looking for something to eat. "That doesn't look very comfortable." Dad was rubbing his neck from having fallen asleep in the chair.

He moaned. "When did I get this old?"

"Seems to me it's been happening a little bit each year," I said, wondering why adults even ask questions like that. He just looked at me, deciding whether or not he wanted to debate the issue.

"Very funny. What are you doing up so early?" he asked, heading to the kitchen to make coffee.

"It's not that early, Dad. It's 8 o'clock. The real question is, where is everyone else?"

It was unusual for everyone to oversleep, but I enjoyed it when I could get it.

"What?!" Suddenly he was wide awake.

"You know. In the morning. Comes after 7?" I resumed rooting around in the refrigerator for milk.

"Oh no. I overslept. I should already be at the office." He hurriedly stuffed all of his paperwork in his briefcase and ran out the door without bothering to change. "Tell your mother I'll call her later." He rushed out the dojo to the garage, jumped in the car, and drove away.

"Huh?" I looked up realizing he'd said something, but he was already gone. I wandered to the living room intending to eat my cereal in front of the TV and sat down in the chair that my dad had just vacated. I pushed the folders he'd left on the table onto the floor and put my cereal down while I hunted for the remote. "We need a remote to find the remote," I mused to myself as I got down on my hands and knees to look under the chair. Just then I noticed that the folders lying on the floor all had names at the top with six-digit numbers. "Hmmmm. Wagner 10-1670. Marlin 10-1671."

I opened up the one that said Marlin on the top and began to read the details of Mrs. Marlin's missing ring.

"WHATDYA GOT THERE?"

"Huh? What? Nothing," I said automatically.

"Why do you look so guilty then," my mom said entering the room.

"I don't know. I'm cursed with a weak gene pool?"

My mom ignored me and took the folders from my hand. "Where'd you get these?"

"They were on the floor. I found them." Even though it was the truth, I still felt guilty. "I think Dad forgot them. Should we call him?"

"Probably," but she was barely listening, already looking around the kitchen trying to decide what to make for breakfast.

Well, I tried. I decided to keep reading until she told me not to. Hmm...A diamond necklace? They discovered it was a fake almost by accident. The chain that the diamond had been hung on was a 24-karat gold chain, and the victim was allergic to anything less than that. When the thief exchanged it, he replaced the chain with a 14-karat chain, and the owner had an allergic reaction.

"So, I think I need to go back to the Tennis Club today and talk to Coach Mike," I was talking out loud, but more to myself than to her. I was surprised when I heard her reply.

"That's what I think, too."

"Huh?"

"You might as well get whatever this is out of your system," she looked at me. "Just be careful and be back by 10 a.m. Take your phone."

I raced to the garage to grab my bike before she could change her mind.

CHAPTER TWENTY-FOUR

"Excuse me," I said to the girl at the desk.

"Yes?" She looked up from the book she was reading.

"Do you know where I could find Coach Mike?" I asked.

"Folding towels. That way," she pointed.

"Thanks." I headed off in the direction she pointed. I saw the coach up ahead who had temporarily stopped folding towels. "Excuse me, Coach Mike?"

"Yes?" He looked up from what he was doing. "Can I help you?"

"I'm Detective Hill," I said, using my most official voice. "I'd like to ask you a few questions. Do you have a minute?" His curiosity got the best of him.

"ALRIGHT, I'LL BITE. ASK AWAY, KID."

I pretended that he hadn't just dismissed all my authority with the word "kid," and continued, "Well, there has been a string of thefts recently, and we've been able to trace them back to your club." I waited to see what effect my words had on the coach. Coach Mike just stared at me blankly.

"What's that got to do with me?" he asked.

"Well, it seems that each one of our victims attended a birthday party at which you were the magician."

"That so?"

"Well, I understand that you do a disappearing jewelry trick. Is that right?"

Comprehension started to spread on Coach Mike's face. "Listen, kid, not that it's any of your business, but I always give the jewelry back," he said a little defensively. "I don't take it from anyone and not return it. You can ask anyone."

Hmm. Usually at this point in the questioning, my dad said that suspects would start to give off a guilty vibe. But I wasn't really getting that from him. Maybe I just wasn't that practiced yet. "So, if I give you a list of names, can you tell me if you did their child's birthday party, or if their child was at the party?"

"Some of them, probably. But I don't ask for the names of the kids attending the parties, you know." He was getting nervous but took the list of names from me just the same. "I recognize some of them," he said noncommittally.

"So, do you remember if you did the disappearing jewelry trick at each of those parties?"

"Sure I did," he said, "It's my grand finale. That's the best trick I have, why?"

"Well, don't you think it's a big coincidence that each of the women that you did the disappearing jewelry trick to, ended up having a piece of jewelry stolen, but replaced with an exact replica?"

"Yeah, that sure is strange." Coach Mike sat there, appearing equally as confused as I felt, but he offered no alternative explanations. Usually, according to my dad, criminals have worked on their plausible deniability and would have been offering suggestions as to what might have "really" happened. But the Coach had an authentic look of confusion on his face. "Why would someone want to frame me?" he asked.

"Frame you?" Seconds after I said it out loud, I said it again to myself, "Frame him? Nah, why would anyone want to frame him. He's just a coach." To Mike I said,

"I'M NOT CHARGING YOU WITH A CRIME RIGHT NOW. BUT IF I WERE YOU, I WOULDN'T GO ANYWHERE, AND I WOULD STOP PERFORMING THAT TRICK FOR A WHILE."

"Gee, thanks, kid." He rolled his eyes at me. "But I have a birthday party this afternoon, and I don't have any other tricks to replace it, so you might just have to arrest me. I just started doing magic about six months ago, so I haven't built up my repertoire yet. If I don't do this trick, then it's pretty lame."

"You're right," I offered. "It's pretty lame. Go ahead then. Just don't leave the state."

"Uh, okay, I'll try not to." He went back to folding towels. "Kids," he muttered under his breath.

This was a strange turn of events, so I thought I would go by the rooms to see if I noticed anything unusual. I didn't really expect to find any evidence, but maybe being in the environment would make me look at things from a different perspective.

I DIDN'T SEE ANYTHING UNUSUAL AS I APPROACHED THE ROOMS.

There was only one entry door to each room, and on each door was posted a schedule of events to take place in that room.

I could hear tennis instruction being given on the courts to the left. I glanced in that direction and saw that on three of the eight courts, instructors had classes of various sizes and were giving lessons. As I looked down the hallway, I saw one of the janitors mopping the floors. His back was turned to me, but I could see that it wasn't Mark, the boy I'd seen previously. This boy was taking care to get into every corner. He seemed to be going painstakingly slow and would glance toward the doors of the private rooms with every glance making sure that he got as close to the doors has he could with his mop. He leaned his mop against the wall and grabbed a rag that had been hanging out of his back pocket. With care, he began to polish the door handles of each of the rooms.

"Now that's what my mom and dad would call work ethic," I thought as I watched him go about his work. I, on the other hand, would be looking for ways to shorten the task, maybe by finding a rug to sweep the dirt under for example. This kid was really making it tough for the rest of his coworkers with his ridiculously high standards. He was so engrossed in his work that he barely heard me tromping down the hallway toward him and he jumped a little bit as I cleared my throat.

"Excuse me, young man," I said smiling.

"Yes?" the boy grabbed his broom, shoved the rag back into his pocket, and resumed mopping. He looked around to see if my dad was with me. His eyes darted around nervously as if he had just been caught with his hand in the cookie jar.

"You're doing a fine job, young man." Wanting to put the boy at ease, knowing that some boys this age were just uncomfortable around girls, I said, "What's your name?" Right after I said it, I saw the panicked look on the boy's face and realized I must have sounded just like my dad when he was beginning an interrogation. He was just a kid after all; couldn't have been much older than me. He was probably sixteen but looked like he was about 13; slightly taller than me, he was probably about 5'7" tall, and weighed about 150 pounds. He had brown shaggy hair and was in need of a haircut. It was just long enough that it fell down over his eyes when he looked down, and he could peer up at people without making eye contact. I got the feeling he kept it long just so he could hide behind it.

"Uh, Steve, why?" The boy was clearly uncomfortable.

HE SUDDENLY LOOKED NERVOUS AND TRIED TO GATHER HIS CLEANING SUPPLIES BEFORE I COULD ASK ANY MORE QUESTIONS.

"Have you worked here long?" I asked.

Steve hesitated. He looked as if he might actually make a run for it. "About a year." He didn't offer any details and busied himself mopping the floor again.

I couldn't think of any more questions to ask him, so I finally gave up. I turned away from him to study the list on the door of the room he'd just been in front of. At the top, it simply said "schedule," and then in order of date, it listed the last names of families scheduled to use the room, and what event they had planned. Next to each family it had the initials MP, NP, or LP.

"Hey, Steve," I called to the janitor.

"Do you know what these initials stand for?"

"No idea," he barely looked at the list.

I guess I couldn't expect him to know. He was just the janitor after all. I read the rest of the names and cross-referenced some of the dates and names with those on my list. I then went to the other rooms to check out those schedules too. Knocking lightly on the door to make sure I wasn't interrupting something, I turned the knob and entered the room. It wasn't currently decorated for any event and was pretty plain. The room contained white walls, void of any pictures or other decorations, as well as a long banquet-style table in the middle of the room. It was surrounded by uncomfortable-looking folding chairs.

"There are no other entry doors to the room," I mused. "So, if it was the magician, he couldn't have handed anything off to an accomplice. He would have had to use the equipment that he brought to the party and snuck out the real jewelry either in his clothing, or with his equipment. This wouldn't have been hard to do," I reasoned.

"Well," I knew the Andersons that were scheduled in about an hour for the next party. I'd have to call my mom and let her know that I was staying for a party!

CHAPTER TWENTY-FIVE

My dad was approaching the front desk, when he saw me standing there talking to the manager.

"Thanks for your time," I said as the manager retreated to the back office.

"What did you find out?" he asked, a little annoyed. I wasn't sure if he was annoyed that I was there, or that I was there first.

"Well," I told him about the initials on the door, "The girl behind the desk told me that the initials indicate whoever is scheduled to do the party." I looked at him triumphantly. "Simple, huh?" I continued, "So MP stands for Mike Price, and LP stands for Lori Peters, the manager," I nodded in the direction of the woman I had just been talking to. "And NP stands for Not Provided."

My dad looked confused, "Not Provided? What does that mean?"

"It means that whoever rented the room was providing their own entertainment, and it was Not Provided," I emphasized these words, "By the club." I walked off in the direction of the party rooms.

"WHERE ARE YOU GOING, YOUNG LADY?"

"Well, it would seem to me," I said, "That the next step would be to see if the parties where jewelry was stolen all had the initials MP after them." His mouth dropped open a little, but he hurried after me.

We poked our heads into the Anderson party. Turns out my dad knew Mr. Anderson. "Hi, George," Paul called out to my dad, as he welcomed kids to his son's party. "C'mon on in, stay awhile," he said gesturing us both into the room. I think he needed a little help.

"Hi, Paul," Dad called back, "Don't mind if we do. We're thinking of having a party here soon, and wanted to check it out," he lied.

"C'mon on in," he laughed. "Don't be surprised if I put you to work though. My wife was supposed to be here too, but she got sent out of town last week, so I'm on my own. She tried to call the club last week to reschedule, but they didn't have another day open. Truth be told, I'm glad for the moral support. I'm afraid I've never done one of these before."

After a few minutes, it was evident that Mr. Anderson had no idea what he was doing. My dad and I scurried around directing activities and serving cake as if the party were our own. "How does this always happen," I thought to myself. "First Mrs. Marlin's party, and now this." Finally, after what seemed an eternity, it was time for the magic act.

"Hey, kids!" Coach Mike burst into the room full of enthusiasm. He stopped short when he saw my dad. My dad's detective badge was visible on his belt, and the Coach was suddenly very nervous.

"Pretend I'm not here, kid," my dad said. He knew that nothing would happen while he was standing there but wanted to see the act anyway. He leaned back, confident that nothing of Paul's would be stolen, but had noticed a fairly expensive-looking pinky ring on Paul's finger when they had shaken hands.

HE WAS SECURE IN THE KNOWLEDGE THAT THE RING WAS SAFE, AND HE WAS GOING TO GET A FIRSTHAND LOOK AT THE MAGIC TRICK.

Coach Mike, realizing there was nothing else he could do, continued with his act. After a few minutes of awkwardness, he got into the flow and soon forgot about his unwanted audience. The kids laughed at all of the "kid jokes" built into his routine and seemed to like the card tricks which, by Coach Mike's own admission, were kind of lame. Finally, it was time for the grand finale.

"And now," he said as if he were the great Houdini, "It's time for my disappearing act." He waited while the kids looked at each other excitedly. "No," he said knowing what they had guessed, "I'm not going to disappear." They looked slightly disappointed. "But I will make something disappear." He appeared to look around the room. "It's got to be something small." He looked at my dad, then at Mr. Anderson. His nervousness had reappeared.

"How about my little brother?" one of the kids shouted, while all the others laughed.

"Still too big," Coach Mike said, still nervous.

"How about my dad's ring?" the birthday boy had spoken up.

Coach Mike and Mr. Anderson both looked nervous at this suggestion. Mr. Anderson started twirling his ring with a nervous laugh, and Coach Mike looked at my dad as if to say, "Is it okay?" My dad nodded to Coach Mike who then looked expectantly at Mr. Anderson.

"Oh, c'mon," he said, "There must be something else you can make disappear? How about this toy ring?" He pulled a plastic spider ring out of one of the goody bags his wife had put together before she left on her trip.

"Well, I think the trick actually works better if people care whether or not the item actually reappears," Coach Mike said looking at the spider ring unenthusiastically.

"C'mon, dad, you're going to ruin my party." He looked at his son and then reluctantly handed Coach Mike his ring. "You better be able to make it reappear," he said almost threateningly.

"Oh, I will. I haven't lost one yet." After another glance at my dad, he went through the motions of his disappearing act.

"…and voila," Coach Mike said, holding the ring in his hand. He looked at my dad as if to say, "See, I told you I'd bring it back," although even he looked a bit relieved to see it. He handed the ring back to Mr. Anderson who immediately put it back on his pinkie finger.

Mr. Anderson looked at my dad. "Whew," he said with a mock wipe of his brow, "That was a close one. That was an anniversary gift from my wife. She'd kill me if anything happened to it." He chuckled nervously but looked like he really meant it.

"WOULD YOU MIND IF I TOOK A LOOK AT IT?" MY DAD ASKED REACHING FOR THE RING.

Mr. Anderson hesitated, but handed it to me to pass over to her for inspection.

"Wow," I said looking at it before I passed it over. "It's an onyx and diamond art deco ring, handcrafted in platinum. It's a European-cut diamond." I looked up and saw my dad staring at me.

"What? I know stuff," I said and looked back at the ring. Apparently, all that time I spent on the internet researching jewelry for Mrs. Marlin's missing ring had paid off. But I wasn't going to tell them that.

"When did you become a master jeweler?" he asked.

I ignored him as if all kids knew those kinds of details.

"It's worth a lot both emotionally and monetarily," Mr. Anderson offered. He obviously appreciated the fact that I had some knowledge of its worth.

My dad took it from me to look it over. It was clear that he wasn't sure what he was looking for, but not wanting to be outdone by a 12-year-old, he studied it anyway. He began to roll it over in his hand trying to see if he would be able to tell the difference between real onyx and fake onyx, or real diamonds and fake diamonds. "I doubt it," he admitted to himself.

"You're probably wondering what the inscription means," Paul said watching my dad study his precious ring.

"Inscription?" I said and grabbed the ring back from my dad. After all, I had it first.

"Inscription?" my dad grabbed it back from me.

"Yes, the inscription." Paul said. "It's kind of hard to notice, but my wife had our initials carved in just behind the setting. It reminded her of the time we carved our initials into a tree while we were dating." He smiled at the thought.

My dad looked again and squinted this time just before I snatched it back again. "Inscription?"

"Inscription?" I grabbed it from him.

"I think we've established that there's an inscription," Mr. Anderson stated.

My dad and I exchanged glances. I knew by the look on his face that he hadn't seen an inscription either. But before jumping to any conclusions, I carefully looked underneath the ring by the setting and held the ring toward the light in case I just wasn't seeing it.

Mr. Anderson looked at us nervously. He saw his ring being passed back and forth but wasn't quite sure what was going on. He grabbed the ring back from them. "See, right here," he said as he turned the ring over. "That's funny," he turned a bit paler as a look of confusion settled over his face. "It looks like my ring, but there should be an inscription right there," he said pointing, "And there's not." These last words came out like a young boy who'd just lost his favorite marble.

I looked at Mr. Anderson with empathy and said, "Ooh...you're in trouble..." knowing that no matter what his explanation was, his wife was going to be mad when he got home. Then, pointing at Mike, I said, "Arrest him!"

My dad glared at me and turned toward Coach Mike. I'd never been present at a crime scene when the actual criminal was committed. This was kind of exciting.

By now, Coach Mike had noticed the exchange and stopped packing his trunk to watch. "Arrest me? Arrest me for what!" He looked visibly shaken. "I didn't do anything. And, as far as I know, you can't arrest someone for crappy magic tricks."

"Yeah, if we could, you'd be in trouble." I looked to my dad. "Aren't you going to arrest him?"

"I'M AFRAID HE'S RIGHT," MY DAD SAID, "WE CAN'T ARREST HIM FOR BAD MAGIC."

My dad seemed annoyed with me. "More importantly," looking back to Coach Mike, "I can't arrest you without any proof."

"Proof?" I said, "You have all the proof you need right in your hand. Mr. Anderson had the ring when he got in here, and now it's a fake, right?"

"Right," he said somewhat confused by the whole exchange.

"Everybody just calm down." My dad held up his hand to Coach Mike in a gesture that said, "Hold on a minute," and explained to everyone, but mostly to me, "I don't have any proof that *he's* the one who took it. We don't know that Mr. Anderson didn't exchange the ring himself right before he handed it to Coach Mike." At this everyone looked accusingly at Mr.

Anderson whose hands immediately went up in the air as if to say, "Hold on a minute, it wasn't me."

"WELL," I SAID, "SEARCH HIM. IF HE HAS IT IN HIS POCKET, DOESN'T THAT PROVE IT?"

I looked at my dad for confirmation. When he didn't answer, I said, "So search him."

"I can't just search him without any proof," my dad repeated. He was speaking slowly as if to a small child. "Unless, of course, he volunteers…" He let his words linger as he looked at Mike.

"Huh?" Coach Mike wasn't sure what had just happened, but now the attention was back on him.

"Would you allow me to conduct a search of your person?" my dad asked patiently.

"Person, what person?" Coach Mike was confused.

I rolled my eyes. "You, he means you! Don't you ever watch *Law & Order*?" I turned to my dad, getting into it now. "Just search him! Don't you have probable cause? Make him spread 'em, and put his hands up against the wall," I said, "Then read him his rights and mirandize him!" I was pretty sure I sounded like I knew what I was talking about.

He turned back to Coach Mike. "So, do I have your permission to search you?"

Coach Mike hesitated but agreed to the search. Looking at the rest of us definitely he said, "I've got nothing to hide." He stretched out his arms and allowed my dad to conduct the search.

After a very thorough search, my dad thanked Coach Mike. "Thank you. You're free to go."

"See," Mike said sticking his tongue out at me. "I told you I was innocent."

"Very mature," I responded. To my dad, I said "Whatdya mean you're letting him go?" I was sure this was the guy. "Did you search him good enough?"

"Of course, I did." He was using his cop voice on me.

My dad turned to Coach Mike, obviously regretting his decision to allow me to tag along on this particular venture. "You're free to go. I have your number if I have any questions." With that, he turned to Mr. Anderson to get more information.

"But..." I protested.

"What?!" Mr. Anderson and my dad said it at the same time, both frustrated that Coach Mike had not turned out to be the guy.

"NOTHING."

Dad and I watched as Coach Mike packed up the last of his things and wheeled his small cart down the hallway. The kids had gotten bored with what had started out to be an exciting version of cops and robbers, but now were playing with some of the toys that Mr. Anderson's son had gotten for his birthday. We watched the boys and then turned our attention back to Coach Mike's dwindling figure down the hallway. It was nearly one o'clock, and a quiet time of day at the club. Aside from the boys in the room, the hallway was mainly quiet. We stepped into the hallway and shut the door behind us to block out the sound of the boys playing.

I tried to come up with an alternate explanation for what had just happened, before my dad started treating me like a kid again. We stood there staring after Coach Mike, listening to the buzz of the clock on the wall above our head, and the sound of the swishing mop as Steve the janitor cleaned the floors in anticipation of the next crowd. Finally, we looked at each other and admitted, at least temporarily, defeat. We returned to the room where we knew Mr. Anderson would need help not only cleaning up, but with the story he was going to have to tell his wife when he got home.

CHAPTER TWENTY-SIX

I was minding my own business, content to eat a bowl of ice cream and watch TV, when my mom came into the room and plopped down on the couch next to me. We sat there in silence for a few minutes.

"I just can't figure out what went wrong," I wondered out loud. "I was so sure it was Coach Mike."

"So, what are you going to do about it?" she asked.

"What do you mean, do about it?"

"WELL, IF YOU'RE GOING TO BE A DETECTIVE, YOU CAN'T GIVE UP AT THE FIRST ROADBLOCK, CAN YOU?" SHE WAITED.

"I guess not."

"So, tell me what happened?"

"What do you mean what happened? Nothing happened. Dad searched him. He didn't have the ring. He didn't do it." Just then, Dad returned home from work. Looking frustrated, he pulled all of the files out of his briefcase and laid them out on the kitchen table.

"Time to start at the beginning," he said and pushed up his sleeves as he went over the contents of the first file.

I sat down next to him. "Well," I said, looking at his timeline. "The crimes had started about six months ago, just about the time that Mike had begun working for the Tennis Club. That's kind of a coincidence, don't you think?"

He nodded in agreement and took out the photos of the first piece of jewelry that had been reported stolen and held it out in front of him. One by one he took the pictures out of their folders and laid them next to each other on the table. "What do they all have in common. What am I missing?"

Normally, he would object to my help, but it seemed like this time he'd resigned himself to the fact that we were in it together.

CHAPTER TWENTY-SEVEN

"So, are these crime photos?" I was puzzled. "Aren't crime photos usually filled with mangled corpses?"

"Only on TV, honey," he shook his head, and went back to his photos.

I picked up one of the photos. "Have you brought these pictures home before?" I asked.

"No, why?"

"I could swear I've seen these before." I glanced back and forth between the two pictures laying on the table in front of me.

"What do you mean you've seen them before?" My mom looked at the photos over my shoulder. "They look a lot like typical jewelry," she offered.

"No, I can't put my finger on it, but these are oddly familiar." I furrowed my brows and got on my deep-thinking look. Frowning, I stared at the photos.

My mom and dad exchanged glances. "So, what are you going to do now?" Mom asked my dad, settling in a chair across from him.

"Not sure." His attention returned to the remaining photos on the table. "There has to be something I missed; I just don't know what it is. Unless Coach Mike ate that ring before he left the room, he's innocent because he sure didn't have it on him."

"I'VE GOT IT!" I CRIED.

"You've got what?" both parents said at the same time.

"Where I saw these pictures before!" I was excited. I knew I'd seen them before.

"Where?" My dad was skeptical.

"On that phone!" Of course, I thought, that explains it.

"What phone?"

"The one at the club!"

My dad stared blankly at me. Then he looked at my mom. "Why don't I know what she's talking about?"

She shrugged her shoulders. "She's your kid," she answered simply and turned back to the photos.

"Alright, Sam, let's start again. Maybe I missed something. What phone at the club?" He couldn't possibly imagine what I was talking about.

I turned to my mom and said, "Remember when I forgot your phone at the front desk?" I waited for recognition to cross her face. "Well, you sent me back in for your phone and I accidentally grabbed the wrong one, remember?" The full impact of what I was saying was starting to sink in. "Well, when I grabbed it, the screen wasn't locked. And, since I didn't recognize the screensaver, I went into the pictures on the phone to see what other pictures you had on it. Remember, I thought it was yours?" I was beginning to backpedal a little wondering if I could possibly get into trouble for what I was about to reveal.

"Go on," my mom prompted.

"Well," I answered, squirming.

"WHEN I CHECKED OUT THE PICTURES ON THE PHONE, I SAW THESE PICTURES OF ALL THIS JEWELRY. THESE PIECES OF JEWELRY."

I pointed at the pictures on the table. "I saw the one of Mrs. M's ring, like you showed me on your phone. And, I just thought you were doing a little pre-shopping for my birthday," I said, "So I didn't say anything." My voice trailed off.

"What are you talking about?" my dad asked, starting to pay attention. After hearing my story, he opened his folders again. "I'll be back later," he said. "I'm going to the office." We stared after him as he walked out the door.

"Um, I think I need to go back to the club. It's still early." Without waiting for her approval, I raced out the door, hopped on my bike, and pedaled toward the club.

CHAPTER TWENTY-EIGHT

"Excuse me," I tried to get the attention of the girl at the front desk.

"Uh, yes," she looked up. "You're back again? Now what?" She sounded annoyed.

"This is official police business, ma'am. I'd like to ask you a few questions if you don't mind." She glared at me and turned back to her work.

"Listen, kid. I don't have time for games," she said.

"This is no game." I waited, but she continued to ignore me. "Can you tell me where Steve is?"

"Well," she said glancing at the clock. "He should just be finishing up, getting ready to go home. You should be able to find him in the employee break room." She pointed to a room across the hall.

Thanking her, I pushed open the break room to find Steve pulling some things out of his locker and putting on his coat. He turned to look at me, then looked behind me to see if my dad was following.

"Hey, Steve," I smiled, trying to put him at ease.

"Hey," he replied looking down.

"I WAS WONDERING IF I COULD ASK YOU A COUPLE OF QUESTIONS ABOUT YOUR PHONE?" I ASKED.

Just then I realized that we were the only two in the break room, and he was a lot bigger than me. "My dad is just parking the car," I lied, "He'll be here in a second."

Smiling, he could tell I was lying, and said "I don't think so, kid."

"I'm afraid I must insist." I stood my ground. "You have pictures of all of the stolen items on your phone. Why?"

He looked startled. "How did you know that?" he began.

"Ah hah! So, you do have pictures of all of the items on your phone," I exclaimed.

"Wait, what?" He was confused. "I thought you already knew that?"

"I knew you had a couple of them for sure, because I accidentally grabbed your phone last week. But you just confessed to the rest." I stood there triumphantly.

"Yeah, but if a bear craps in the woods," he began.

"WHAT? WHAT DOES A BEAR HAVE TO DO WITH THIS?"

"Ugh. If no one heard me but you, it doesn't really count, does it?" Now he was the one who was looking triumphant.

"Maybe," I said, thinking quickly "If I hadn't been recording this conversation." I pulled my phone out of my pocket and showed it to him.

He eyed my phone as if he were going to take it, and I quickly put it back in my pocket. "You're still going to have to stop me," he said. With that he started running toward me.

As he got closer, I reached for his collar, planted my foot in his stomach, and dropped to the ground. With all of the forward momentum he had, Tomoe Nage worked perfectly. He crashed to the ground, knocking over the trash can in the process. Just as I jumped to my feet, my dad walked through the door.

"YOU ARE HERE," I EXCLAIMED IN RELIEF. "STEVE JUST CONFESSED TO THE CRIMES, AND I HAVE IT ALL ON TAPE." I HELD UP MY PHONE FOR PROOF.

My dad looked at Steve, not exactly sure what had just transpired. "Is this true?"

"Yes," Steve suddenly broke down like a scared teenager rather than a hardened criminal and started bawling. "I did it. I confess! My cousin is in the jewelry business," he said as if that explained it. "I started to notice that a lot of these rich members took their expensive jewelry off before they worked out. They would just leave them in their lockers." He shook his head. "Since the club supplied all the locks for the lockers, I had all the combinations. All I had to do was open the locker, snap some pictures, and close the locker back up before they got back. Nothing was ever disturbed, and nobody ever got hurt. Right? Once I had the pictures on my phone, I could just send them right to my cousin. He could make an exact replica, and I could replace the jewelry the next time that person was in the club. See?" He paused like he was waiting to be congratulated. When none came, he continued. "It was perfect. The members had been taking their jewelry off for so long when they worked out, they didn't even recall doing it when it came time to fill out a police report. That part always got left out. And when the magician started doing the disappearing magic trick, he seemed like the perfect fall guy. Nobody gets hurt."

"Huh? You mean, except for the part where an innocent man could have gone to jail for a really long time for something he didn't do? Just because you didn't physically harm anyone in your crime didn't mean people didn't get hurt," I said.

Ignoring me, he said, "Like I said, if that lady wouldn't have had her ring cleaned, and you," he glared at me, "wouldn't have grabbed my phone, I would have gotten away with it."

MY DAD GOT OUT HIS HANDCUFFS.

CHAPTER TWENTY-NINE

"See, if it wasn't for me, you would have never solved it!"

"Yes, you're a genius," both parents sounded exhausted, but were too tired to argue.

"YOU COULDN'T HAVE DONE IT WITHOUT ME," I PERSISTED.

"Next time you'll have to let me look at the evidence sooner in the case, so I can help you solve it quicker."

My dad just groaned but smiled at the same time. "Nice work, Sam," he admitted, "but I think your Tomoe Nage could stand a little improvement. In fact, let me show you what you could have done if he'd have tried to tackle you instead."

I looked at him, mildly interested. "We call it Tawara Gaeshi. Rice Bag Reversal. C'mon into the dojo. You get to be the rice bag."

DOJO RULES

KARATE BOW (REI) ETIQUETTE

1) BOW BEFORE YOU ENTER THE MAT.

2) BOW TO YOUR PARTNER BEFORE TRAINING.

3) BOW TO YOUR PARTNER AFTER TRAINING.

4) WHENEVER YOU'RE NOT SURE, BOW.
   (BETTER SAFE THAN SORRY)

5) BOW WHEN YOU LEAVE THE MAT.
   (BUT FACING TOWARD THE ROOM. NOTE: DON'T
   POINT YOUR BUTT TOWARD THE MAT AND BOW.)

OTHER IMPORTANT STUFF TO REMEMBER

6) DON'T CHEW GUM, OR EAT IN CLASS (OF COURSE, DUH).

7) MAKE SURE YOUR GI (UNIFORM) IS CLEAN.
   NOTHING WORSE THAN TRAINING WITH SOMEONE
   WHO'S UNIFORM SMELLS LIKE B.O. (GROSS!)

SAM
HILL

A COUPLE OF BASIC MARTIAL ARTS RULES TO REMEMBER:

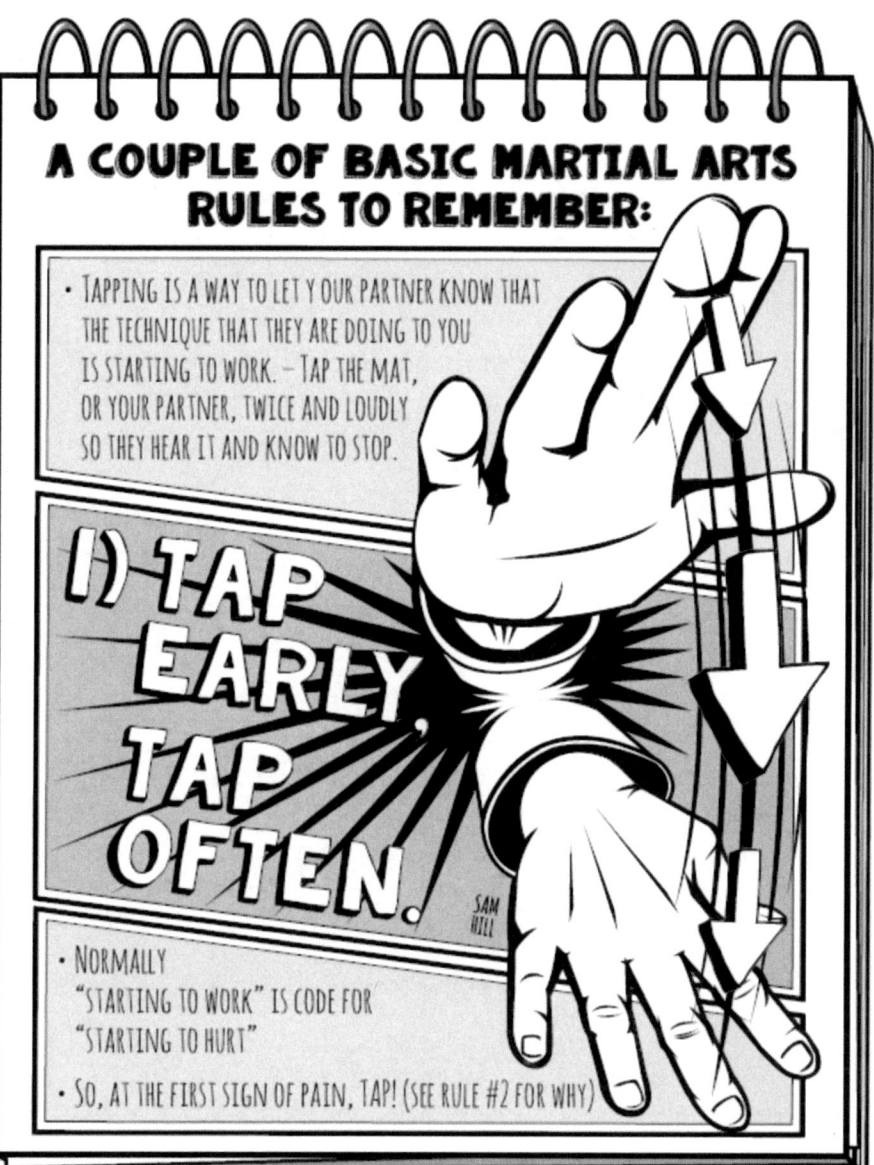

- Tapping is a way to let your partner know that the technique that they are doing to you is starting to work. — Tap the mat, or your partner, twice and loudly so they hear it and know to stop.

1) TAP EARLY, TAP OFTEN.

SAM HILL

- Normally "starting to work" is code for "starting to hurt"

- So, at the first sign of pain, TAP! (SEE RULE #2 FOR WHY)

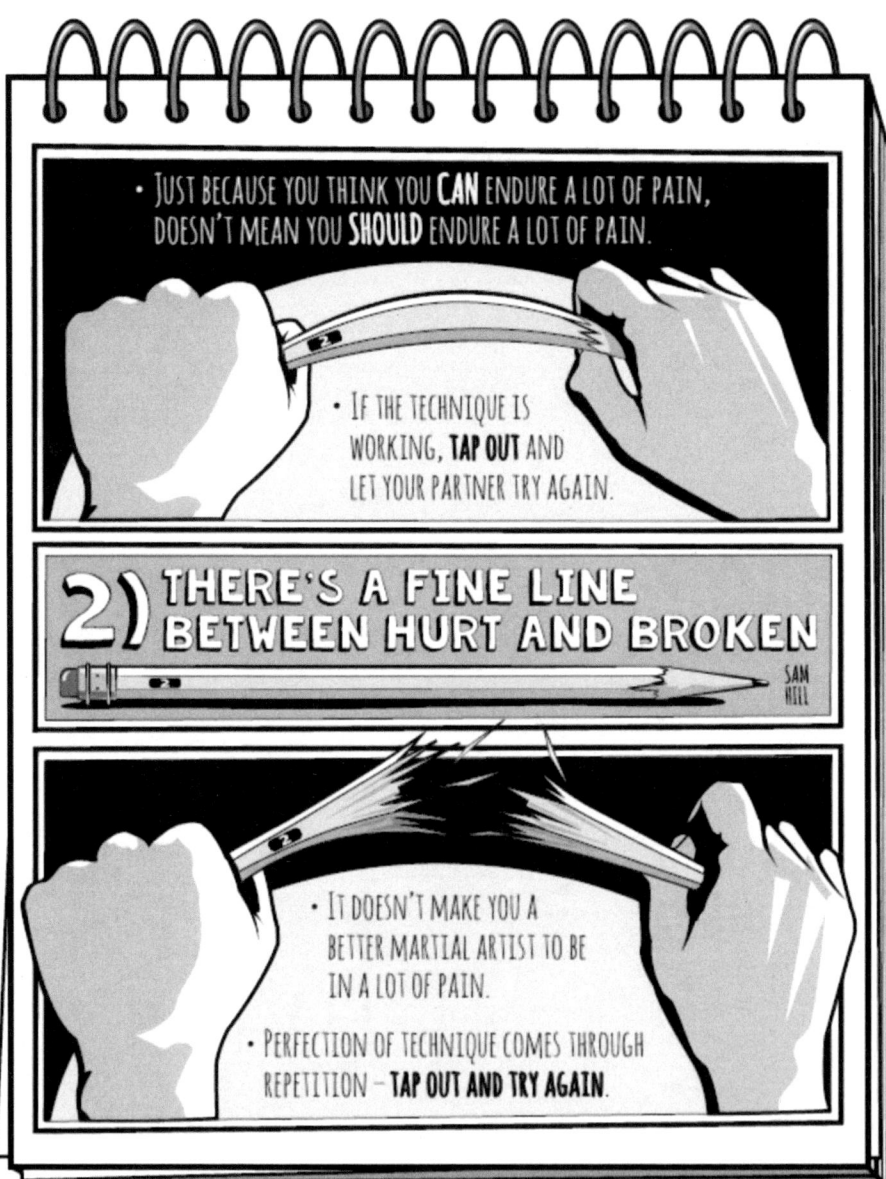

- Just because you think you **CAN** endure a lot of pain, doesn't mean you **SHOULD** endure a lot of pain.

  - If the technique is working, **TAP OUT** and let your partner try again.

2) THERE'S A FINE LINE BETWEEN HURT AND BROKEN

SAM HILL

- It doesn't make you a better martial artist to be in a lot of pain.

- Perfection of technique comes through repetition — **TAP OUT AND TRY AGAIN.**

MARTIAL ARTS TECHNIQUE:

A BREAKFALL IS A WAY TO "BREAK YOUR FALL" WITHOUT BREAKING YOUR BONES. IT'S TAUGHT FROM A SQUATTING POSITION BECAUSE IT'S SCARY TO DO IT FROM A STANDING POSITION.

1) STEP BACK AND LOWER YOURSELF TO THE GROUND

2) TUCK CHIN IN TOWARD CHEST

3) TUCK TAILBONE – LAND ON BUTT (NOT TAILBONE) AND ROLL BACK

4) HIT THE GROUND AS HARD AS YOU CAN BEFORE YOUR SHOULDER BLADES HIT

5) RECOVER ARMS QUICKLY (DON'T LEAVE THEM ON THE GROUND)

BREAKFALL

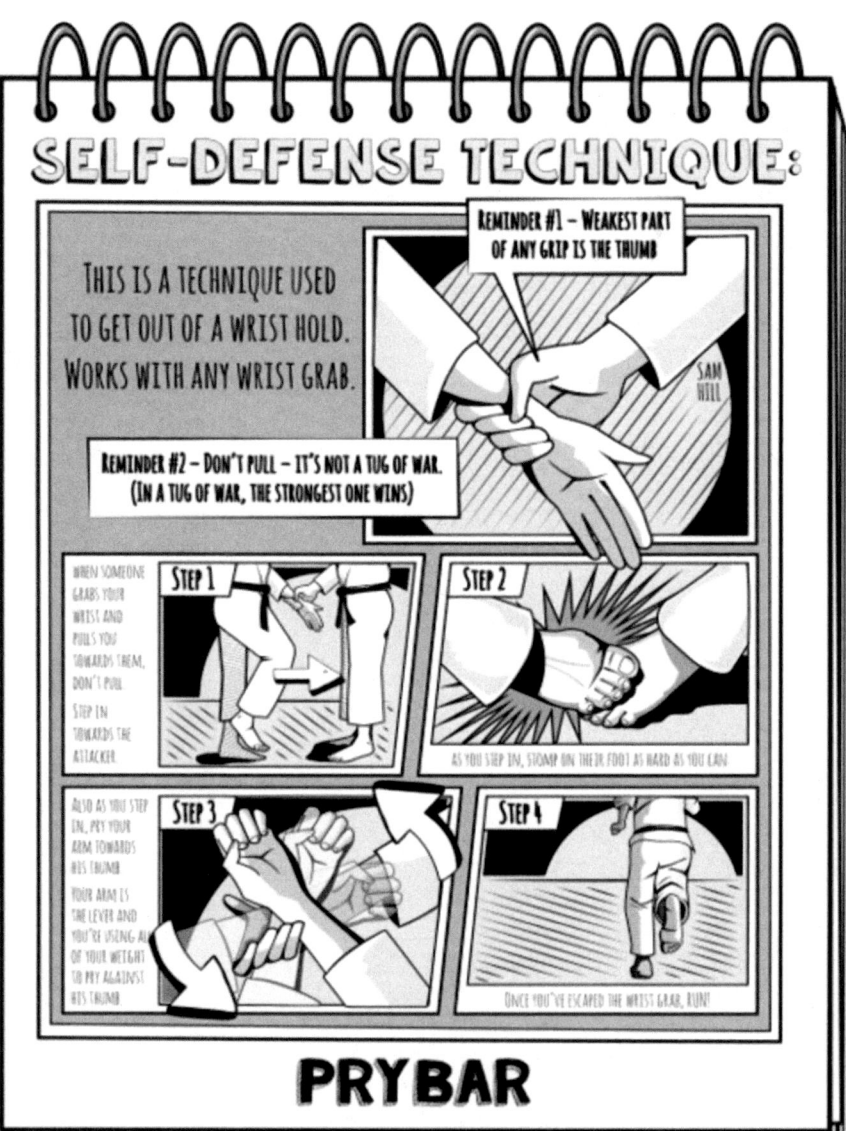

PRYBAR